THE
HOUSE
WITH
THE
GREEN
ROOF

THE HOUSE WITH THE GREEN ROOF

Ashish Vikram

PARTRIDGE
A Penguin Random House Company

To order additional copies of this book, contact
Partridge India
000 800 10062 62
orders.india@partridgepublishing.com

www.partridgepublishing.com/india

Contents

To,
All the people who have laughed with me before

Foreword by the Author

This started out as the screenplay for a movie. A Bollywood suspense movie complete with its own *signature suspense tune* (which is of course a must for any suspense movie worth its salt), a glamorous heroine, a dumb hero and the mandatory song to release the pressure whenever the suspense started to show any signs of building up. I had barely gotten through the first couple of chapters when I realized that I did not know how to write a screenplay! I did not know how to write a book either but I figured that I had at least read a small number of books in my lifetime. I had never so much as seen a screenplay before. A small calculation by my sharp IIT brain and I concluded that I was infinitely more experienced with books than with screenplays. So this book further degenerated from the Bollywood screenplay it was supposed to be into a book of the yet to be made Bollywood film. The glamorous heroine and the dumb hero stayed in place. Thankfully I found it rather difficult to play songs in the middle of a book and so, some of the mandatory songs went away. But the movie camera still lurks behind every corner and the *signature suspense tune* keeps popping up in the most inopportune places.

I believe you can enhance your enjoyment of this book by creating a picture of the movie scenes in your mind as you read it.

Chapter 1

Leaving IIT

The *signature suspense tune* played for a brief while as the camera panned over the majestic main building of IIT Delhi with its parabolic roof and the big bell on top. As the camera zoomed in, the scene below the main building started coming into focus. One could see a long row of student cycles parked below, a little way away from the main building. The camera moved towards them.

Two students were examining the cycles one by one. They seemed to be looking for a particular one.

"Can't you at least remember which side you parked it?" asked one of them sounding somewhat exasperated.

His friend, Veenu thought about it again. He always parked his cycle somewhere in the long row of cycles they were now examining. At least whenever he was at the insti he parked it here. Otherwise he parked it in the hostel parking lot. So the cycle really should have been here unless...

A ramshackle looking Maruti 800 car with some paint peeling off and a dent in both the front and back bumpers was parked a little distance away. The front of the car was facing away from Veenu and his loyal friend. The balding man in the driver seat was not in a good mood. Every few seconds, he turned his head and glared angrily at the two boys. The background music changed to the *signature suspense tune* whenever this man was in the picture.

"Do you think my cycle has been stolen again?" Veenu asked. So far they have been stolen at the rate of one per year. All my scholarship money has gone into buying cycles. Final year had gone well so far, but now just as I was about to graduate, it looks like I have lost another one."

They continued to do a sequential search through all the cycles in the long row.

Veenu looked closely at the last one in the row, probably hoping that closer scrutiny would turn into the cycle he was looking for. This was his last chance anyway. It did look somewhat similar to his cycle. He held it up. His friend looked on hopefully. But it was not to be. Veenu let go of the cycle in anguish. It fell over against the cycle next to it. Veenu quickly caught it and prevented it from falling down again. But it was too late. The second cycle in the row had already fallen onto the third cycle. Veenu and friend watched in horror as the domino effect chain reaction caused all the cycles in the row to fall over one by one, with a continuous clattering and clanging noise. A few bemused passers-by stopped to watch the spectacle. The man in the car winced and covered his ears with his hands as he too watched the scene. The noise stopped when every last cycle parked there had fallen over entangled with the one next to it. All but one of course, since Veenu was holding on to the first cycle he had saved from falling, rather tightly. The passers-by continued on their way, not bothered by the scene they had just witnessed.

"Oh God" groaned Veenu and friend simultaneously, shaking their heads as they realized what they had to do next. They set about the task of straightening the cycles one by one.

"That man in the car" said Veenu's friend in a hushed voice. "Why is he going on staring at us?"

"Don't know" said Veenu lifting another cycle.

"Do you think he is the cycle thief?" asked the friend.

Veenu stared at the car for a while, his mouth was open.

"That is not the cycle thief" he said. "That is my dad!"

Veenu's friend dropped the cycle he was picking up. "Your dad?" he said.

"Yes" said Veenu "I did not come here on my cycle at all! Dad had said he would pick me up. You pick up the cycles. I have to run." He ran off in the direction of the car.

"Hey!" started Veenu's friend but Veenu had already run off. He sighed as he surveyed the long line of fallen cycles. With a resigned look, he set about the task of picking them up.

A breathless Veenu opened the passenger door of the Maruti 800 and sat down.

"Sorry Dad" he said, putting on his seat belt. "The cycles had fallen down."

Dad turned the ignition key to try and start the car. The engine whined but did not catch. Veenu waited patiently. The car started on the third attempt. Dad hunched close over the steering wheel and started to drive through the IIT campus. "I noticed the cycles falling" he said sarcastically. "But what were you doing out there for so long before that? I have been waiting here and you were busy chit chatting with your friend."

"My friend could not find his cycle" said Veenu. "I was helping him look for it. We were afraid it had been stolen."

"All your friends are just as careless as you" snorted Dad.

They passed the library building and started to approach the down ramp close to the hostels. There were gardens on both sides. A peacock strolled nonchalantly across the garden on the right. Male students with cloth bags hanging from their shoulders could be seen walking along the roads. Some were on cycles. Female students were conspicuously absent. A solitary girl was walking down the down ramp. Such high quality eye candy was obviously a rarity in these parts and most people seemed to be looking at her. One fattish guy on a cycle sped down the ramp looking sideways at the girl. The guy on foot coming in the opposite direction did not appear interested in looking straight either.

The cyclist was just a few feet away from the guy on foot. They were about to collide! Instinctively the cyclist turned his head to look straight. He veered and braked, hard. His cycle screeched and stood up on the front wheel. He had managed to avoid hitting the pedestrian! However he himself went flying into the air and landed just in front of the guy on foot. The cycle followed and landed on top of him. The guy on foot continued to walk, looking sideways. He collided with the fallen cycle and fell on top of it.

Other students, both on foot and on cycles glanced momentarily at the scene of the two fallen students at the bottom of the ramp, sandwiching a cycle. But this was obviously not as interesting as the girl so they went back to looking at the girl. Father and son drove along, also looking at the girl. They continued on as the two prostrate students managed to disentangle themselves and got up, dusting themselves.

"What happened about your job? Asked Dad as the car went up the up ramp.

"I have accepted the Bangalore job" said Veenu slowly, looking sheepish.

"The Corn Systems one?" Dad exclaimed and shook his head disapprovingly. They were now driving past the hostels towards the hostel gate. "If you had to go to Bangalore, you could have joined some good Company. There are so many good Companies in Bangalore. There is Info Systems. There is Wipro. But you! You did not listen to anybody."

Veenu did not reply. There was a long pause

"And what does this Corn Systems do? Do they make corn flakes?" asked Dad.

Veenu waved to some friends loitering outside the *dhaba* and looked wistfully at it. "No" he said. "It is a software company. It's a startup. They are opening a new office in Bangalore. They are working on some very interesting fail safe security software."

Dad did not look impressed.

"The pay is good" Veenu continued hoping to impress his dad. "They have promised to provide a laptop even before I join. They will have it delivered so I can start learning even before I have officially joined. They are providing me with free accommodation in a nice guest house in Bangalore for two months until I can find an apartment of my own." He paused slightly. "And they have a rather nice logo."

"They have a nice logo?" asked Dad somewhat encouraged.

"Yes" said Veenu. "You know it is a really nice long yellow corn on a cob," he said trying to trace the outline of a corn with one hand. He did this by moving a partly closed fist up and down a few times along the imaginary long cob. "A lot of skin is open at the top with nice ripe yellow corn sticking on it" continued Veenu with a dreamy expression in his eyes. A thought blurb showing the bright yellow/green corn on the cob logo appeared above Veenu's head. Dad looked horrified. His eyes widened. A thought blurb with a "censored" sign appeared above Dad's head. He banged his head on the steering wheel. Only a slight movement of the head was required to achieve this banging since he was hunched close to steering wheel with his head just inches from it.

Dad shook his head disapprovingly. "Hmmph. Corn Flakes Systems," he exclaimed with scorn.

The car passed through the hostel gates and dangerously entered the immense traffic on the main road outside without waiting for a gap or slowing down. The car immediately behind them braked hard to avoid a collision. It screeched to a halt inches from the Maruti 800. The second car behind it honked loudly but also managed to brake hard and screech to a stop without hitting anything. The driver of the second car was particularly pleased at being able to stop just inches from the car in front of it and folded his hands in thankful prayer. But the car driver behind him was not as alert. He started to brake hard but was too late. He skidded into the car with the praying driver. The second car lurched forward and crashed into the first car. It was now badly dented from both ends. Meanwhile several more cars behind them were honking, braking, skidding, screeching and banging into cars in front. There was a huge pile up. A crowd gathered, tempers flared and a screaming match ensued. Meanwhile father and son seemed completely oblivious to all the noise and chaos behind them. The Maruti 800 continued to drive on with no addition to the dents it already had. There was no change in the expression of either father or son.

Chapter 2

Off to Bangalore

A song, "The Destination is Not Far Now" was playing in the background.

Veenu was sitting at home. The bell rang. It was a courier. Veenu's package from Corn Systems had arrived. It was immediately obvious that the package was from Corn Systems because the packaging had a big bright yellow and green corn on the cob logo on top. Veenu eagerly opened the package and removed his new shiny black laptop from it. Shiny black that is, except for the Corn Systems corny bright yellow and green logo sticker right across it. Veenu's mother smiled, a warm broad smile reflecting both love and pride. His father could be seen in the background closely examining the logo which covered the entire packaging with a frown on his face.

The background score was still playing – "The Destination is Not Far Now."

Veenu was sprawled on the floor in front of his laptop. A worn out copy of "Fundamentals of Data Structures and Algorithms" by Horowitz and Sahni was next to him. Veenu's sister, a girl of about eighteen was sprawled beside him engrossed in her book. He was reading his email excitedly. His e-ticket to Bangalore had arrived. He pumped his fist and said "yesss!" Veenu's sister peered into his laptop screen and saw the ticket. She held up her hand for a high five. Veenu's hand met hers with a loud clap.

The background song continued.

Veenu and family were at the airport in front of the departure terminal. There was a spring in Veenu's step. He looked handsome and somewhat muscular in his T shirt and slightly frayed blue jeans. His sneakers must have been white at some point in time but at this point were mostly a light uneven shade of brown. His prized Corn Systems' laptop was in his backpack. An old looking suitcase was in the trolley in front. The frayed copy of "Fundamentals of Data Structures and Algorithms" was still in his hand. He hugged his Mom and shook his Dad's hand. His sister waited her turn but then clasped him in a tight hug. Veenu looked around slightly embarrassed to see if anybody was watching. Some people were! He pushed his sister away quickly. Veenu's Dad waved goodbye with a slight tear in the corner of his eye. His mom's eyes were shining brightly and she had a smile on her face. She looked much younger than Dad although they were only a couple of years apart.

Veenu walked briskly inside the terminal building. Several air hostesses were walking across, in single file. They were all smiling at him. Had he been staring at them? Veenu smiled back embarrassed again.

The camera captured the classic shot of Veenu's plane taking off. As usual this shot clearly meant that Veenu was on his way.

Veenu was sitting next to the window. His table was open. The "Fundamentals of Algorithms and Data Structures" book was open on it. A fair, stern looking man in a full formal dark blue suit and red tie was sitting next to him in the middle seat. The center of his head was bald and shone slightly. There was a circle of reddish grey hair all around the central bald patch. This hair pointed straight upwards and increased in length as it went away from the bald patch. The top view of the man's head showed a circle of hair which sloped gently down into the central shiny bald patch. It looked like a volcanic crater! One could be forgiven for expecting lava to start spurting out any moment.

The background song had paused.

An airhostess handed Veenu his food tray with a big smile. Veenu's movements were somewhat robot like. He picked up the plastic packet containing the cutlery. There was a pause. Then a sudden movement caused the plastic packaging to tear completely and the plastic cutlery to scatter onto the plate. There was a pause in movement again. The Lava Crater Head Man in the suit was leaning forward and staring intently at Veenu's food tray. His own food tray was still untouched on his table.

The *signature suspense tune* had started. Veenu's hand moved to the plastic wrapping on his main dish and paused. A sudden movement and the plastic wrapping was gone. A pause followed by another quick movement and the plastic wrapping on the salad disappeared. There were a couple of button tomatoes in the salad plate. Perhaps Veenu had not seen a button tomato before. He was poised with a fork over one of them rolling it slightly back and forth. The man in the suit stared intently. A sudden quick movement caused the fork to plunge into the button tomato. A stream of juice spurted out of the tomato and headed straight for the man in the suit. Veenu looked at the man. His face was covered with a streak of tomato juice that started from his forehead and went down across his largish nose, lips and chin and ended on the knot of his tie. There were a few tomato seeds mingled with the juice.

"Sorry" said Veenu. He handed him the tissue from his plate. The tissue was still within its plastic envelope. The man in the suit accepted the tissue and wiped his face with it without bothering to take it out of the plastic. The juice spread more evenly all across his face and forehead.

Beautiful Bangalore: Veenu's plane was above Bangalore airport. The airport with open green spaces all around and the highway leading into it looked beautiful from the air. The airport looked clean and beautiful to Veenu as he walked through the aero bridge. He had slowed down to let the Lava Crater Head Man go in front and was now some distance behind him. The tomato juice on the Lava Crater Head Man's face had dried up by now but several seeds were still stuck to his forehead and nose. Somehow the comical face and hairstyle of this man did not do justice to the formal suit beneath, which looked rather incongruous. Veenu got the Lava Crater Head Man out of his mind and concentrated on the eye candy around him. There was no shortage of eye candy in this part of town!

Veenu walked into an airport taxi. The camera moved up to show an aerial view of the beautiful highway leading out of the airport with manicured plants on both sides and palm trees in the central median. Veenu was fascinated by the city and looked around intently. The taxi took the on ramp onto National Highway 7.

They soon went past the white Windsor Manor building that looked like a castle with the golf course right opposite it and were in the heart of the city, driving past Vidhan Soudha. This is the seat of power in Bangalore with architecture from India's colonial past.

The road entered Cubbon Park, that big park right in the center of town. Several purple Jacaranda trees were in full bloom inside the park. And as is customary for Bangalore's flowering trees, not a single leaf was visible on them which were completely covered with purple flowers. Bangalore has a pleasant climate all year round which somehow seems to encourage the growth of trees. Perhaps that is what causes so many different varieties of flowering trees to bloom so profusely that there is no room for any leaves during the bloom. Veenu had never seen something like this before.

The taxi passed the bright red, round public library within Cubbon Park, went past the Bamboo Grove and emerged on to Mahatma Gandhi road. The camera moved upwards to give a grand aerial view with the Cricket Stadium followed by the Army Gardens and Parade Grounds. Ulsoor Lake was visible on the far left. It was amazing that there could be so much open space in the heart of a major city. A train was just entering the elevated metro station on MG road. The right side of the road was lined with shops.

As they made their way through Inner Ring Road a view of the Embassy Golf Links software park came up with the golf course on the left, and modern office buildings on the right with iconic names such as Microsoft, Yahoo, IBM and Dell clearly visible amidst the palm tree lined avenues.

Soon after, Veenu noticed tall stone walls protecting what appeared to be a large forest behind them. An obscure sign claimed that this was one the campuses of the Indian Space Research Organization. "An aptly named organization" thought Veenu judging by the amount of space they had to themselves in the middle of the city. He knew of course that Bangalore was home to several of India's premier space and defense research organizations. Presumably there was an office building somewhere in the middle of the jungle behind the walls.

The taxi was now getting closer to the International Technology Park or ITPL which was to be Veenu's final destination.

The phenomenal growth of the software industry in Bangalore over the last couple of decades has necessitated the creation of some large office complexes to cater to the ever growing demand for quality office space. ITPL was one of the first such complexes to be set up but is possibly still the largest and most important. It is built on 28 hectares with 6 huge glass front buildings set amidst landscaped gardens. These buildings together have almost 2 million square feet of office space. On a typical week day each building has between 4,000 to 5,000 IT professionals working inside.

Veenu's taxi had finally reached the main entrance of ITPL. Veenu was anxious to report to work but first he had to deal with *security*. The taxi was not allowed to go in. So Veenu had to remove his bags from it and let it go. Then Veenu was not allowed to enter either since he did not have a valid company picture id card.

"But I am joining today" pleaded Veenu. He showed them his appointment letter. The security guard disappeared for a long time with his appointment letter. He eventually came back with a burly supervisor. The supervisor had several questions for Veenu but finally asked him to enter his name in the visitor book and enter. His bag would have to remain with security and could be collected on the way out. The backpack was allowed in but he was directed towards the X ray screening area.

Veenu walked towards the screening area which was to the right of the gate. He noticed that cars that were allowed to enter the premises based on the ID check at the gate were sent off to a separate area towards the left of the entry gate. All cars were thoroughly screened for bombs using various kinds of detectors. This was more than the cursory check of the boot that was common at most places.

People coming out of the car park area joined Veenu in the X ray screening queue. His laptop had to be removed from the laptop bag and passed separately through the X ray machine. But even that was not enough. All new unregistered laptops had to be powered on and booted to show the security guy that it really was a working laptop. Most employees had learnt not to carry their laptops or any other bags around to speed up the security. Even so Veenu really wished that Microsoft had worked a little more on the boot up time of their OS. There was a long line of people waiting as their laptops were booted up slowly. It took Veenu half an hour just to get through that line. The registration number of Veenu's laptop was noted down. He was told that it would be verified when he brought it back out. Veenu himself had to go in through a metal detector and also frisked. "This is worse than an airport!" thought Veenu. Despite the obvious inconvenience to the employees, he appreciated the real checking going on here and thought it appropriate for protecting one of the IT icons of the city.

Then there was another long line for checking computer equipment being delivered to ITPL. Veenu noticed boxes with the unmistakable bright yellow logo of Corn Systems being unloaded from a tempo trailer. A few desktop computers, again with the bright yellow logo painted on their sides were lying on wheeled bases besides the trailer. Veenu ran towards the trailer.

"Computers for Corn Systems?" he half said, half asked the man who was opening the box that he had just unloaded from the truck.

"Yes" said the man suspiciously looking up towards Veenu.

"I work there" said Veenu proudly showing the man his appointment letter.

The man smiled. "Good Company" he said. "They have sent computers in a wheeled base so it is easier for us." He pointed to one of the computers lying on the ground in its wheeled base.

"Why are you unpacking them here?" asked Veenu.

The man shook his head. "It is so painful to deliver computers to ITPL" he lamented. "We have to unpack them all here then wait in line forever for them to be checked. Do you know, they put each computer on and wait for it to boot! I wish Windows would boot up faster." The man smiled at Veenu. "But at least your Company sends computers with wheels so we don't have to carry them around."

Veenu patted his shoulder. He understood the man's pain. He felt prouder than ever that he had decided to join this Company. But he could not hang around here forever. He needed to hurry to his new office.

The 6 main buildings inside ITPL are arranged in U shaped groups of 3 buildings each. The Innovator, Discoverer and Explorer form the first 3 older set. The Corn Systems office was on the 2nd floor in the Innovator. Veenu walked over to the center of the U. The three buildings towered over him. Someone had clearly taken a lot of care to lay out the small garden in the center of the U with green and reddish black shrubs laid out in wide alternating strips, cut close to the ground. Veenu had been impressed as he drove through Bangalore but was even more impressed with ITPL. Despite the intense security required at the entrance, he was really looking forward to working here.

Veenu walked towards the entrance of the Innovator looking upwards and feeling tall and light even though he was dwarfed by the buildings. As he lowered his eyes to look towards the entrance, he suddenly did a double take and ducked instinctively. There with his back towards Veenu, it was unmistakably the Lava Crater Head Man! He was clearly impressed by this place too for he was looking upwards, photographing the Innovator with his mobile phone. Veenu straightened himself up. Why had he ducked? True, he had drenched the Lava Crater Head Man with tomato juice in a streak all the way from the top of his forehead down to his formal tie, and nobody could be expected to be happy about that but the Lava Crater Head Man really was not a threat and there was no need to be alarmed. Perhaps it was just that Veenu had been busy looking up at the buildings and the sudden appearance of the man in his sight had alarmed him. Still Veenu did not really want to say "Hi" to the Lava Crater Head Man and cleverly avoided his eye as he quickly entered the Innovator and made his way inside.

Veenu stood in the corridor outside the office of Corn Systems. The entrance to the reception had glazed glass walls and a glass door, with the bright yellow "corn on the cob" logo covering the glass door from top to bottom and "Corn Systems" written in bright yellow on the glass walls. Veenu admired the logo with pride. A red LED blinked on top of the glass door and the security camera positioned there moved to focus on Veenu.

The *signature suspense tune* had started.

Did Veenu need an access card to enter? He did not have one. Veenu hesitated but then he pushed the glass door. It swung open. Veenu entered what was to be his office. It was somewhat dark inside with an eerie multicolored glow cast around the room by blinking yellow and green LEDs. This light was coming in through another partially glazed glass door beyond which some computer equipment (perhaps an internet router thought Veenu) had several blinking LEDs. The light was being scattered by the glazed glass and cast a rather sinister glow of dim light in the room. Veenu's eyes took a few moments to adjust to this dim light. This was the Corn Systems reception. There was a sofa for visitors and a reception table with a desktop computer on it. The Corn Systems logo was painted on its side. A uniformed security guard was sitting on the chair behind the reception table. His head was resting comfortably on the table and he was snoring peacefully. Veenu approached the guard.

"Hello", he said meekly. There was no effect and the guard continued to sleep.

"Hello", said Veenu again, this time in a much louder voice. Still no effect.

Veenu frowned and shouted loudly "HELLOOOO".

The guard slowly opened his right eye and looked at Veenu. Something must have registered through the one open eye for he now opened his other eye. He had noticed that someone was there but was in no hurry. He yawned and slowly pulled himself up to a sitting position.

"Yes" he said. "Why are you shouting so much?" He flicked a switch and the room was suddenly brightly lit.

"Ummm" said Veenu. He blinked in the sudden bright light. He took out his appointment letter from his backpack and handed it over to the guard. The security guard looked at the name on the envelope but did not bother to open it.

"Yes" he said. "This company has shut down. Everybody has left."

Veenu stared at the guard not quite getting it.

"I have an envelope for you" said the guard.

A bewildered looking Veenu watched as the guard opened a drawer in the desk and pulled out an envelope.

"Yes" he said. "Here it is."

He handed over the envelope to Veenu. The bright yellow corn on the cob logo was printed in the top corner. Veenu opened the envelope and took out the letter inside. It was an official letter on the company letterhead with the bright yellow logo. Veenu quickly glanced through the letter.

"Dear Veenu," it said, "The founders of the company needed to part ways due to personal reasons…. The investors decided to exit… We are very sorry for the inconvenience…" Then towards the bottom of the letter it said, "A check for 6 months of salary minus applicable taxes is enclosed as your severance."

Veenu fished inside the envelope and took out the check. He stared at it. That was quite a bit of money. Corn Systems was clearly a generous company with big hearted founders. He would really have enjoyed working here. He felt sad that the Company had shut down before he could start contributing. He also felt somewhat guilty that he was getting a fat check for doing nothing but accepted it nevertheless. He addressed the guard. "What should I do with this laptop?" he asked pointing towards his backpack and expecting that he would have to return it since it was Company property.

The guard shrugged his shoulders. "I don't know" he said. "Do whatever you want."

The guard yawned. It was a big yawn. He looked sleepy and bored. Veenu was not sure what to do next. Did he have a place to go to?

"What about my guest house" he asked aloud.

"Guest house?" repeated the guard looking puzzled. "What guest house?"

"My guest house" persisted Veenu. "The company had given me a guest house to stay in Bangalore for two months while I looked for my own apartment."

The guard shrugged his shoulders. "I don't know" he said.

Veenu stood still looking at the guard. The guard was getting ready to sleep again. "Ok" he said waving Veenu away.

Veenu started to turn around. But what was that? Had he just seen the shadow of a man on the glass door to the room with the computer equipment? The *signature suspense tune* which had stopped a while back started again as he turned and stared hard at the glass door trying to look beyond it through the unglazed portions. But there was nobody there.

"Who is inside?" said Veenu directing his question to the guard.

"Inside?" repeated the guard. He was getting impatient with Veenu's questions.

"Inside that room" said Veenu pointing towards the glass door.

The guard shrugged his shoulders. "Nobody" he said.

Veenu was still staring at the door.

"Ok" said the guard loudly. "Now go." He waved at Veenu to leave.

Veenu shook his head. The blinking lights had been playing tricks on him. Slowly he turned around and made his way out. The guard's head was already on the table. He had switched off the lights. Veenu could hear a snore as he walked out of the door.

Chapter 3

The House with the Green Roof

Veenu's auto, that three wheeled vehicle that was ubiquitous in Bangalore, stopped in front of the Corn Systems' guest house. It had a beautiful stone wall with butch work all around. Bougainvilleas in different colors were hanging over the walls from inside and covering nearly half of the outside walls. As is characteristic of Bangalore, there was hardly a leaf visible on the Bougainvillea which was full of brightly colored flowers. Some pink, some orange, some yellow and some white. Veenu paid the auto and approached the black gate of the bungalow. The gate was a little lower than the walls and made of wooden strips painted black. Behind the gate a pretty house was visible. It was made out of red wire cut bricks, partly covered with dark green ivy. It had a sloping roof covered with clay tiles in a slightly lighter shade of green. "The Greens" read the sign on the wall next to the gate.

There was a green colored (matching the roof) security outhouse on the right side of the gate. Veenu approached the outhouse. A guard in blue uniform was sitting inside it looking through the visitor's window. This guard was actually awake!

Veenu tried his usual technique. "Hello", he said meekly.

"Yes" said the guard sounding very much like the other guard Veenu had encountered. He even looked similar! But no, this one was awake and so was obviously not the same man.

Veenu was ready with his appointment letter. He handed it over to the guard wondering whether he was still allowed to stay here.

"Yes" said the guard. He looked at the name on the appointment letter. "Veeeenu" he said. He pulled out a long register and fingered through the names. His finger stopped on the name "Vini". "Veeeeni" he said slightly puzzled. He looked at the appointment letter again. "Veeeenu" he said. He looked back at the register. "Ahhh", he said relieved. The name right after "Vini" was "Veenu".

"Room No 3" said the guard.

He removed a key from its place on the wall and handed it to Veenu. "Your room key" he said. "Go in and turn right."

"Thank you" said Veenu feeling relieved.

"For the front door" said the guard handing him another key.

"Thank you" said Veenu again. He hesitated for a moment. "Ummm" he said.

"Yes" said the guard.

"Vini is also staying here?" asked Veenu. He had noticed the name in the register.

"Yes" said the guard. "She is in room number 1. For your Company."

"For *my* company?" had Veenu heard right?

"Yes" said the guard. "From your Company. She came yesterday."

"Ok" thought Veenu. "This was also a new employee of Corn Systems."

Veenu was not good at names. Particularly names of girls. None of the girls in school talked to him because he was forever confused about their names and frequently referred to them by the wrong name. If there was one thing Veenu had learnt in high school, it was that girls liked to be called by their own names! He did not have the problem of calling the girls in his class by the wrong name in IIT. Of course that was mainly because there were no girls in his class at IIT so he could not call any by the wrong name.

He was determined to remember his colleague's name correctly. "Vini" he said aloud in an attempt to remember the name as he walked towards the gate dragging his suitcase behind him. "And I am Veenu." That similarity in names should certainly help him remember. "Vini, Veenu" he repeated aloud.

Veenu opened the gate and walked inside. The gate opened into a cobbled stone footpath leading up to the house. Veenu stopped for a few seconds to admire the view. The cobbled stone path was lined with red terracotta pots on both sides which had different colored Honeycomb growing in them. Each of the plants was topped with brightly colored Honeycomb flowers. There were deep red, yellow, purple and deep orange Honeycomb. Beyond the Honeycomb was green Carpet Grass with more flowering plants along the walls which were almost fully covered with Ivy. Bougainvillea flowers in different colors brightened the top of the walls. These same flowers had been visible from outside. The corner to Veenu's right had a Bamboo grove in it. There was a water body with a rock formation in front of the Bamboo grove. Water cascaded unevenly down the rocks into a small fish pond below. There were brightly colored gold and yellow fish cavorting in the pond. They looked like giant goldfish. The fish pond was lined with round pebbles at the bottom. In the front, the green tiled roof sloped down to just below the door level. The final portion of the sloping roof would form a shelter for someone standing in front of the door.

"Vini, Veenu. Vini, Veenu" Veenu continued his memory exercise as he entered *the house with the green roof.*

The door opened into a large dining area with a big wooden dining table in the center with a few chairs around it. Beyond the dining table, in the right corner was a wooden staircase presumably leading up to guest rooms on the 1st floor. On the left of the dining area was the lounge with a large TV screen and comfortable sofas. Veenu turned right as instructed. This led him into a short corridor. The door for room number 3 was at the end of this short corridor. Veenu turned his key in the door lock and entered the room. It was a tastefully furnished room. There was a low bed in the center. A flat screen TV was on the wall in front of it. A light wooden writing desk with a reading lamp was next to the TV with a wooden chair in front of it. There was a large window above the desk which looked out into the garden beyond. Veenu could see the Bamboo grove, rock formation and fish pond outside through the window. There was a side table on each side of the bed with a lamp placed on it. A wooden cupboard was inserted in the wall on the other side of the bed. Veenu was quite pleased with his room. He entered and closed the door behind him.

He needed to check something on the net. He sat down on the desk and took out his Corn Systems laptop and started it up. The login screen appeared. Veenu logged in. Was there any *wifi* in this place? There was. Veenu connected to the unsecured network called "Guest House". It did not require a password. He was on. He went to the Corn Systems website. It was still there with no sign of the Company having been shut down. He went to the "Executive Team" page. The photographs of both the founders showed up along with a short write up. The founders were Sammy Batra and Suresh Sharma. Of course Veenu already knew that. Sammy Batra had brought in the management skills and roped in the investors and also brought in security expert Suresh Sharma into the company as a co founder. Suresh Sharma had a PhD thesis on developing failsafe security systems that could take appropriate action even in the event of such failures as a power system failure or the internet connection breaking. Veenu googled Sammy Batra. Nothing significant came up. There was a link to his Linked In profile and a few links to some news articles about his founding Corn Systems and a link back to the Corn Systems website. Veenu then googled Suresh Sharma. There were obviously lots of Suresh Sharma's out there. A lot of links came up that seemed to have nothing to do with the Corn Systems' founder. Veenu googled "Suresh Sharma Corn Systems". Yes, now he got the right Suresh Sharma. Again there was a link to his Linked In profile and a few links to news articles. The most recent news article, just a few days old, was interesting. In fact, it was really interesting! Veenu clicked on it. "Suresh Sharma, security software expert and co-founder of Corn Systems found dead" it said. The co-founder of Corn Systems had committed suicide by hanging himself from the ceiling of his apartment in Silicon Valley. A suicide note had been found. Apparently Suresh was having some personal problems or in other words, girlfriend trouble.

"What a waste" thought Veenu. "The security expert had been unable to secure himself from his own mind. Anyway, that explained why Corn Systems had been shut down."

Veenu realized that he really was out of a job. The six months salary he had gotten was a nice bonus but he still needed a real job. He logged on to his email account and downloaded his resume. He would need to start sending it out to various Companies.

Veenu emerged from his room a little while later. He was still in the same jeans but had changed his T shirt. His hair was slightly wet. "Vini, Veenu, Vini, Veenu" he muttered under his breath. He was looking for room number 1. He walked past the dining and lounge area into the short corridor on the left of the main entrance. Sure enough the door at the end of that corridor had '1' written on it. Veenu stood in front of the door and contemplated his next action for a while. He finally knocked. A girl of about 22 opened the door. She was wearing a loose fitting, short sleeveless T shirt which extended just below her belly button. A short pair of tight form fitting shorts and a pair of pink sports shoes with socks that barely made it above her shoes completed her meager attire. With great difficulty

Veenu managed to bring his eyes to be level with her face. God, she was amazing! Veenu opened his mouth but no words came out. The girl smiled at him. Veenu tried again. "You are Veenu?" he said.

"No" said the girl matter of factly. "I am Vini".

Veenu stared at her not sure what to say next.

"But perhaps *you* are Veenu" continued Vini. "I have been waiting for you."

"W..Waiting for *me*?" said Veenu taken aback. His eyes went up and down again. "In these clothes?" he wanted to say but instead he said, "How did you know that I was coming?"

"When I checked in yesterday" said Vini in her matter of fact tone. "I asked the security guard if anybody else was here from Corn Systems. He told me that you were going to come today."

Veenu was impressed.

Vini smiled at him. It was a beautiful smile. "There is nobody else here to talk to" she said, "except for an inscrutable Japanese Gentleman. I guess he is the strong silent type. He does not say anything. He only bows when he sees me." Vini bowed as she said this in a good imitation of the Japanese Gentleman. Veenu got an eyeful of cleavage as Vini bowed.

Veenu's head reeled. Still, he was desperate not to be put in the same category as the Japanese gentleman. He was thinking hard. What should he say next? Instead he found himself bowing in an involuntary response to Vini's bow.

Vini giggled. "You seem to be just like the Japanese Gentleman" she said.

"Come in" said Vini before Veenu could come up with something to say. She went inside her room. Vini's room had exactly the same furniture as Veenu's. Vini sat comfortably on one of the sofa chairs next to the side table. In the meantime, Veenu had come in about two steps into the room and stood uncomfortably next to the door.

Vini looked at Veenu. "Come in some more" she said.

Veenu moved in a couple of steps more into the room.

"Sit" said Vini gesturing to the bed in front of the sofa chair.

Instead Veenu moved towards the wooden chair next to the desk. There was a newspaper lying on the desk. "US warns of terrorist threat to IT infrastructure" read the headline. "Lokayukta police raids sitting MLA" read the headline next to it. Veenu pulled out the wooden chair. He turned it towards Vini and perched himself rather uncomfortably on one half of the chair.

"Did you meet Sleeping Beauty?" asked Vini.

"Sleeping Beauty?" asked Veenu who's immense IIT brain did not seem to be working very well at this time.

"The Corn Systems security guy" clarified Vini.

"Yes" said Veenu comprehending.

"So?" continued Vini. "Did they give you six months' salary?"

"Yes" said Veenu again. There was a pause. "Did they give you six months' salary too?" asked Veenu brightly.

"Yes" Vini nodded.

There was another pause. "So" said Vini. "When are you treating me for getting your first salary?" She looked at him expectantly.

There was another pause. Veenu's head was still spinning. "Should we go for dinner?" he said finally getting up from his chair as if he was ready to go right away.

"Yes. Lets" said Vini in her matter of fact tone. "But first I was about to go the gym."

"Gym?" said Veenu sounding very surprised.

"Yes. Gym" said Vini looking at herself and in a tone that made it clear that this should have been obvious from the clothes she was wearing.

Veenu realized that perhaps she was dressed for the gym but was lost for words again.

"Why don't you also come?" said Vini. "This place has a great gym. These Corn System guys have arranged everything for us."

"Ok" said Veenu.

Vini got up and started to walk out. Veenu followed. They walked together towards the gym with Vini leading the way.

"I wish this Company had not shut down" said Vini. "It would have been great to work for them. But still. At least they have given us six months' salary. And it seems like we can stay here for the full two months that we were promised earlier. The guard does not seem to have any idea that Corn Systems has shut down."

"Are you a software engineer" asked Veenu suddenly.

"No" Vini smiled. "I am an HR specialist."

By now they were in front of a door that said "Fitness Center".

Vini pointed at Veenu's jeans. "Jeans are not allowed in the gym" she said.

"Oh" said Veenu looking at himself. "I will be back in a minute." He ran off towards his room.

Vini went inside the gym.

———◆———

At the gym:

The song "Watching You Watching Me" began in the background as Veenu entered the gym.

Veenu was now wearing loose fitting slacks and a sleeveless T shirt. He did have some amount of muscle. Veenu entered the well equipped fitness center. A universal machine with modules to exercise different muscle groups was immediately in front of the entrance towards the center of the area. A Japanese Gentleman was on the Chest Press. He had huge bulging muscles. Veenu looked at himself. In spite of having a decent body, he looked puny in front of the Japanese Gentleman. The metal pin was inserted to select the maximum possible weight on the machine. The Japanese Gentleman's rather large chest stuck out as he had taken in a deep breath and was ready to lift with the full strength of his substantial muscles. The normal expression of the Japanese Gentleman's face gave the impression of a slight scowl. This turned into a bigger scowl as Veenu entered the gym. The Japanese Gentleman liked his privacy and could do without this intrusion into it while he was trying to further build his already substantial chest muscles. He would have preferred the gym all to himself but there was already that girl on the treadmill, who to the Japanese Gentleman's great dismay was always smiling at him forcing him to bow to her each time. The Japanese Gentleman was definitely much happier in *the house with the green roof* two days ago… before it was overrun by these kids.

The treadmills were at one end of the gym facing a wall completely covered with a mirror. In fact most of the wall space in the gym was covered with mirrors so that you could look at any part of the gym from almost anywhere, either directly or in one of the reflections. The girl who was always smiling at the Japanese Gentleman was on one of those treadmills. Veenu headed towards an empty treadmill next to her.

Vini must have been on the treadmill for a few minutes already. She was perspiring slightly and her clothes were sticking to her because of the wetness. Her shapely shape was well defined in the sticky top and shorts. Veenu could not help staring at her as he climbed on to the treadmill. "She is beautiful" he thought. Vini turned her head towards Veenu. He looked rather lost, and sweet, thought Vini. She whistled at him. "Hello good looking" she said.

Veenu had just switched on the treadmill but Vini's whistle caused him to forget to start running along with the moving belt. His feet went backwards along with the belt and slid off it. His hands were still holding on to the handle bars in front. He was now in a strange stretched position with his feet on the floor just behind the treadmill and his hands hanging on to the handle bars in front. There seemed to be no way for Veenu to get off the machine or get back on. If he left the handle bars he would fall down face first onto the running machine. He surveyed the moving belt below him with concern.

Vini watched, rather amused. She gasped suddenly, for Veenu had let go off the handles and was falling, face first, towards the belt below. But Veenu's arms came down under him and his palms hit the belt first keeping him from hitting his face on it. For a moment, he looked as though he was doing a *push up*. His arms moved backwards with the belt while his feet remained firmly implanted where they were on the floor so that he was soon in a 'bent over touching his feet' kind of position. Who said that the only exercises possible on a treadmill were walking or running? Veenu straightened himself as his hands reached the edge of the machine.

Vini, who had been quite concerned for a bit, clapped. "Bravo" she said.

Veenu took a bow. He jumped back onto the running machine and tottered backwards but managed to get his feet moving just in time to prevent himself from getting thrown off it again. He increased speed and got himself to the center of the machine and caught hold of the handlebars in front. It had taken him a little longer than normal, but he was now finally in the correct position on the treadmill and walking as he was supposed to.

The Japanese Gentleman who had briefly interrupted his routine to watch Veenu, scowled further. He had not appreciated Veenu's calisthenics on the treadmill!

Veenu tried to keep his eyes on the handlebars in front of him but they soon darted to Vini's beautiful form at his side. Unfortunately Vini's eyes met his and Veenu quickly brought his eyes back to the handle bars. Vini laughed. What a beautiful laugh it was. But what was she laughing for? Veenu concentrated harder on the handle bars.

Vini was almost done with the treadmill. She got off it and headed to the corner to get an exercise mat. Veenu really had no wish to be on the treadmill and got off it too. He would rather be on one of the weight machines. Vini was in the floor space between the treadmills and the weight machines. She was bent over unrolling the exercise mat. He quickly went past her to the Universal Machine. He decided to start with the knee and thigh exercise and sat on the bench meant for this.

Vini was standing on the mat and doing military school style aerobic exercises to the lively beat of the music (Watching You, Watching Me). Each time Vini jumped and moved her arms up, her T shirt rode up a few inches.

The Japanese Gentleman sat on the bench next to Veenu ready to exercise his shoulders. The pin was inserted to select the maximum possible weight. This was the first time that the Japanese Gentleman was going to do the shoulder exercise with that much weight. His hands clutched the handle bars ready to lift. He closed his eyes and took a few deep breaths summoning all his strength.

In the meantime, Veenu finally remembered that he was sitting on this bench to exercise his legs. He moved his ankles behind the pads and lifted his feet with some force to counteract the weight he was expecting. But Veenu had forgotten to insert the pin. There was hardly any counter force and Veenu's feet moved up with great speed. Surprised, Veenu quickly brought his feet back into the normal sitting position. The single metal weight attached to the pulley mechanism that had gone up with Veenu's feet movement practically fell back on the other metal weights below. There was a loud 'Claanggg' as metal hit metal. The sound reverberated through the large room.

The Japanese Gentleman opened his eyes with a start, jarred out of his concentration. He could most certainly do without these clanging noises while he was trying to further build his already substantial shoulder muscles. He turned and glared at Veenu.

"Sorry" said Veenu embarrassed. What would Vini think? He looked towards her. She had stopped jumping up and down and was smiling indulgently at Veenu. This time Veenu smiled back.

The Japanese Gentleman shook his head. He must not let these minor worldly distractions spoil his concentration. He closed his eyes and took a deep breath both to calm himself down and get the required oxygen to his shoulder muscles as he got ready for the lift again. His massive chest heaved as it filled with air.

Veenu needed to insert a pin in the appropriate weight before he could continue with this exercise. He turned and looked behind him. There was one inserted in the weights next to his. He removed it.

The Japanese Gentleman took a final deep breath. He grunted as he put all the strength of his substantial shoulder muscles into the lift. But there was no resistance to the Japanese Gentleman's mighty heave. His arms went straight up at high speed jarring his muscles. Confused, he opened his eyes and let go of the handle bars in alarm. The single weight attached to the pulley mechanism that had gone up when the Japanese Gentleman had heaved upwards fell back on the other metal weights below. There was a very loud 'CLAAANGGGGG'. The Japanese Gentleman closed his ears with his hands. He was sure he had inserted the pin to select the maximum weight. He looked behind him to check. Veenu was frozen like a statue with the pin in his hand just about to insert it into the weights for his own leg exercise.

"You!!" said the Japanese Gentleman severely. He scowled, his biggest scowl ever, at Veenu. Veenu, still frozen, looked back sheepishly at the Japanese Gentleman. The Japanese Gentleman snatched the pin out of the motionless Veenu's hands.

There was a sound of laughter. Both Veenu and the Japanese Gentleman turned around to see Vini on the floor holding her stomach and laughing uncontrollably. She had been laughing for a while but when Vini is really laughing hard her laugh goes silent so they had not heard her so far.

The Japanese Gentleman was disgusted. He had had enough of trying to further build any of his already substantial muscles with these two around the place. He got up, gave a menacing glare to Veenu and stomped off towards the change rooms. Halfway there he realized he still had the metal pin in his hands. He stopped suddenly and turned around to glare at Veenu. He threw the metal pin at Veenu forcefully. The projectile hurtled towards Veenu's face. Veenu caught it cleanly.

"Thanks" said Veenu. He bent back and inserted it into the leg exercise machine.

The Japanese Gentleman muttered something in Japanese and stomped off towards the change rooms.

Vini did not bother to get up from the floor after her laughing bout. Instead she sat on the exercise mat her legs stretched out in front of her. Veenu was finally exercising his legs in the Universal Machine. Vini bent over and touched her toes. She had a very flexible body.

Veenu moved to the chest press, the one that the Japanese Gentleman was on when Veenu had entered the room and lay down on the bench.

In the meantime Vini had wrapped herself up around a big exercise ball. Her waist was on top of it with her legs wrapped around it in front and her toes touching the floor. Her hands were touching the floor behind the ball. She really was flexible.

Veenu could see Vini in the mirror in front of him and was having a difficult time concentrating on the chest exercise he was supposed to be doing. He tried to push up on the handle bars with some effort. They did not budge at all. He tried again a little harder, his muscles strained but the handles did not move. Veenu sat up and looked behind him at the weights. The pin was still where the Japanese Gentleman had left it on the bottom weight. No wonder Veenu could not lift it. He adjusted the pin to select a smaller weight.

"Bye" said Vini smiling at Veenu as she crossed him and headed towards the shower room.

Veenu had not seen her coming towards him and was startled by her "Bye".

"Bye." Veenu managed to smile back at her. Despite the distractions, he had managed to get in some exercise. He was sweating and needed a shower. He did not want to look as if he was leaving the gym just because Vini had left so he did a couple of sets of the shoulder exercise alone in the gym. The background music had stopped. He did not like being in the gym alone. He left quickly for the shower room.

The Japanese Gentleman must have taken a long shower for he was still in the Men's changing room wrapped in a towel, taking some clothes out of an open locker. Veenu avoided looking at him. He grabbed a towel and headed into one of the shower rooms.

Veenu just needed a short shower and was out in a couple of minutes wrapped in the towel, his clothes in one of his hands. He was still wet. He kept his clothes on the bench below the lockers. The locker right in front of him was open. There was something shiny inside it. Veenu looked more closely. It was a watch. Veenu took it out and examined it. The strap consisted of two golden dragons, their mouths holding the watch. Their tails could be entwined together to lock the watch on the wrist while wearing it. The watch face had jewel encrusted markings and golden hands.

"The Japanese Gentleman must have left this behind," thought Veenu. "Maybe he is still around."

Veenu ran out of the change room, still in his towel, water dripping from his body. He went out of the gym and noticed the Japanese Gentleman at the end of the corridor. Veenu clutched his towel with both hands. The watch was clasped in between his hands and the towel. He ran after the Japanese Gentleman.

"Hey" shouted Veenu.

The Japanese Gentleman stopped as Veenu approached him. He looked suspiciously at the strange sight of Veenu running towards him, clutching at the towel around him with wet hairy legs protruding from under it. Veenu stopped in front of him, out of breath from the running. The Japanese Gentleman watched Veenu with arms crossed around his muscular chest.

"Yes" said the Japanese Gentleman.

Veenu first needed to tend to his towel which was no longer tucked in properly and was still around him only because he had been holding it with his hands. The Japanese Gentleman watched with a scowl on his face as Veenu tightened his towel and tucked it back in.

Suddenly the Japanese Gentleman's mouth opened wide. His expression changed to shock. "My watch!" he said pointing to the watch in Veenu's hands.

"Your watch sir" said Veenu handing over the watch. "I found it in the locker in the change room."

The Japanese Gentleman accepted the watch and looked at it fondly. He was overwhelmed with emotion. He bowed so deeply that his head brushed against the towel tied around Veenu's waist. Veenu moved back a step afraid that it would come off again.

"Thank you" said the Japanese Gentleman straightening up.

"You are welcome" nodded Veenu and started to walk back towards the gym.

The Japanese Gentleman examined his watch lovingly. It was inconceivable that he could have forgotten this special watch in the changing room.

The Japanese Gentleman ran towards Veenu. The *signature suspense tune* had started.

"Wait" shouted the Japanese Gentleman.

Veenu stopped and turned around. "What happened?" he asked as the Japanese Gentleman approached him.

"Thank you" said the Japanese Gentleman. He bowed deeply again.

"No Problem" said Veenu. He started to turn around.

"No. Wait" shouted the Japanese Gentleman. He put one arm on Veenu's shoulder to stop him from leaving. "You don't understand. This is a velly impoltant watch. It was given to my gleat, gleat, gleat…" The Japanese Gentleman was counting the number of 'gleats' on his fingers. "Gleat" he continued, "glandfathel by the emperor himself." He beamed at Veenu.

"That's great" said Veenu. He needed to get back to the changing room and get into his clothes. He brushed off the Japanese Gentleman's hand from his shoulders and started walking briskly back.

Veenu glanced back over his shoulders. The Japanese Gentleman was following him! Veenu held his towel with one hand and broke into a run. He rushed into the changing room and bolted it from inside. The Japanese Gentleman was soon outside the change room and was trying the door knob! It was a good thing that Veenu had bolted it.

"They are all mad" said Veenu aloud to himself.

Veenu quickly dried himself and changed back into his gym clothes. The sound of the Japanese Gentleman trying to open the door knob had stopped. But what if he was still waiting outside?

The *signature suspense tune* had become louder.

Veenu bent down and tried to look out from under the door. There did not appear to be anybody there. He unbolted the door half expecting it to be flung open by the Japanese Gentleman. He waited a bit, then turned the door handle and opened the door slightly. He peeked out. He could still not see anybody outside. He flung open the door fully. It was empty outside.

The *signature suspense tune* stopped.

"He's gone" said Veenu relieved.

Chapter 4

Dinner

Veenu was back in his room. He had left his cell phone there. He sat on the bed and checked it now. He had 3 missed calls from *Home*! He had neglected to call home after landing in Bangalore. They would want to know about his new job. What would he tell Dad? His phone rang again. He stared at the display. It said *Home*. His phone continued to ring insistently. He finally picked it up. It was his mother on the line.

"Hello."

"Hello Mom" said Veenu trying to sound cheerful.

"Why didn't you call?"

"I just got home from work. I was about to call" said Veenu.

"How was your first day at work?" asked Mom.

"It was… it was great" Veenu replied.

"Are you settled in?"

"Yes" Veenu replied with more confidence. "They have provided me with a lovely guest house. And my colleagues are really beautiful."

"Beautiful?" asked his mother.

"I mean nice. My colleagues are really nice" said Veenu.

"I am so happy" said his mother. "Listen. Find your own place quickly. Don't stay in the guest house for too long."

"Yes mom" said Veenu.

"Your sister wants to talk to you."

Veenu's sister grabbed the phone. "Hi" she said excitedly.

"Hi" said Veenu.

"Are you behaving yourself?" asked the sister.

"Of course" said Veenu.

"When am I getting my gift from your first salary?"

"Very soon" said Veenu.

"Send it by courier" instructed the sister. "And don't be cheap. You have a real job now. Papa wants to talk to you. Call me later."

Veenu's father had been hovering around in the background looking grumpy. He grabbed the phone. "Is the name of your company really Corn Systems?" he asked.

"Yes" said Veenu "and it is a great company."

"Ok good" said his father. "But I was hoping that the real name of the Company was something else."

"I have to go for dinner now" said Veenu.

"Ok. But keep calling. You know that your mother gets worried very fast" said his father.

"Yes dad" said Veenu. "I will."

"Have… have fun" said his father hesitantly.

"Thanks dad."

Veenu stared at his phone for a while after the call looking thoughtful. He slumped down on the bed. He picked up the TV remote and started flicking channels on the TV staring blankly at it. Lovely images of Vini in the gym appeared before his eyes.

A financial news channel was playing on the TV. "The Sensex went up by 189 points today," said the voice on the channel. Veenu flicked the remote. He was now on a food show. "Now put in a bit of red chili" said the chef. Veenu flicked. He was now on a local news channel. "The Japanese Prime Minister, Shinko Motu San…" Veenu flicked. "… has now started running faster." Veenu was watching a horse race. "He is level with the first horse," shouted the excited commentator. "And Racing Storm has won the race!!" The camera focused on the horse's rear end as he went past the final line. "What a beautiful…" Flick. The horse's bottom transformed into a bikini clad bottom that was sashaying up the ramp on a fashion channel. Veenu sat up slightly. More of the model came into view as she sashayed away from the camera. Flick. "Ummm. What a tasty dish," said the chef licking his fingers.

There was an almost imperceptible knock on Veenu's door. Veenu wanted to lower the volume on the TV instead he had changed channels was now back on the fashion channel where bikini clad girls were walking up and down the ramp. There was a louder knock on the door. The *signature suspense tune* had started. A horrible thought came to Veenu. Was it the Japanese Gentleman? Veenu hesitated but finally got up slowly and opened the door.

It was Vini. Veenu looked relieved. Vini walked into the room wearing a normal T shirt and tight fitting jeans. Even so, Veenu found that he could pay more attention to her face now. She was extremely pretty. Her just showered face looked fresh and bright. She had big black eyes. Her long, slightly wet hair was combed straight back so that her pretty oval face was visible fully without interference from her hair.

"Why did you take so long to open the door?" Vini scolded. "What were you up to?"

"Nothing, nothing" said Veenu quickly. "I… Umm. I was just watching TV."

Vini looked at the TV. A curvaceous bikini clad model had just walked to the end of the ramp and was posing provocatively. Vini gave Veenu an inquiring look.

"I mean" said Veenu. "I was just changing channels and.."

"And the remote got stuck on this channel on its own" completed Vini.

"Yes" said Veenu. "I mean. No."

"What about dinner?" asked Vini.

The image of the chef licking his fingers flashed in front of Veenu's eyes. "D..Dinner?" he said not sure what Vini meant.

"Yes. Dinner" said Vini. "Weren't you supposed to take me out for dinner after the gym?"

"Dinner" considered Veenu.

"Let's go" he said decisively, switching off the TV as he said this. With the TV off, he felt brighter already.

"Where should we go?" asked Veenu. "You must be familiar with the area?"

"Yes" said Vini. "I have been here for two days. I know the area very well."

Veenu looked confused. He was not sure if Vini was being sarcastic or not.

There was a twinkle in Vini's eye. She burst out laughing. What a beautiful laugh it was.

<hr />

Vini and Veenu were soon standing outside a Chinese restaurant. The restaurant was on the roof of a single storey, old colonial house that had been converted into a shop on the ground floor and a restaurant on the terrace. It was on the same street as *the house with the green roof.* This street had houses only on one side. The other side was essentially a large tract of empty unused land covered with shrubs and some trees. It must have been either unused government land, disputed land or land belonging to the army. This part of the street had a few restaurants and shops on it. There was a computer accessories shop on one side of the restaurant and a chemist on the other.

The white restaurant building stood out in the dark. A few cars were parked outside it. The entrance was through a courtyard with a fountain and a few wooden chairs and tables in it. The courtyard led into the main building which had been converted into a shop on the ground floor. The shop had all sorts of eclectic odds and ends in it most of which were hand crafted. It had lovely scented hand made candles with real flower petals visible through the translucent wax, hand made paper in different colors, greeting cards, hand made soap, a few framed paintings, crockery including a beautiful hand painted tea set complete with cups, saucers, a tea pot, milk bowl, sugar bowl and a tea cosy. There was also a solitary drum set and a banjo in one corner of the shop. Vini stopped to browse around a bit. She admired the tea set.

"Lovely shop isn't it?" she asked Veenu.

Veenu was hanging around behind her, his hands in his jean pockets.

"Yes. Lovely" he nodded.

The staircase leading up to the rooftop restaurant was at the back of the shop. They passed the payment counter to get to the staircase. The elderly lady at the counter smiled at them as they passed her.

Vini and Veenu went up the stairs and emerged into the restaurant. Half the restaurant was covered with a terracotta tiled roof supported by black metal pillars while the other half was open to the sky. It overlooked the courtyard below and the street beyond it. Such open air restaurants are quite common in Bangalore where the not too hot, not too cold weather almost throughout the year makes eating outside a very pleasant experience. The restaurant had wooden tables with wooden place mats. The chairs were black wrought iron with thick white cushions. There was a candle lit lantern and a single red rose bud in a slim vase on each table. Overall it had a quaint romantic atmosphere. The restaurant was about a quarter full.

There was a man in a dark blue suit standing just inside the entrance to the restaurant next to the hostess' desk. He was leaning on the desk, facing the restaurant. Veenu approached the man from the back and tapped him on the shoulder. The man had not heard Veenu approach. He jumped and turned around quickly.

"Table for two please" said Veenu in his most sophisticated voice smiling at the man.

The man's mouth opened slightly. He wanted to say something but was not quite sure what. Just then the hostess arrived. She had soft, North Eastern features with wide black eyes and long silky hair and a well defined nose. She was wearing a tight fitting black dress.

"Your table is ready, sir" she said to the man in the blue suit.

The man in the suit followed her to his table in the open air part of the restaurant.

Vini and Veenu waited near the hostess' desk.

"Table for two please" said Vini to the hostess when she returned.

The hostess led them to a table for two towards the center of the restaurant. She pulled out one of the chairs for Vini. At the same time, Veenu attempting to be chivalrous pulled out the other chair. Vini considered her options. She decided to sit on the chair offered by Veenu. He beamed and pushed it back in. Or at least he tried to push it back in but the heavy wrought iron chair with Vini sitting on it seemed stuck to the floor and did not budge. Veenu tried pushing again but there was no result this time either. He tried again. This time Vini helped by lifting herself off the chair just as Veenu started to push. The chair jerked forward a little before Vini landed back on the chair. It was still not fully in, so Vini and Veenu repeated the process – Veenu pushed and Vini lifted herself momentarily and then fell back on the chair. They had to do this one more time before the chair was fully in position under the table.

On the other side of the table the hostess waited patiently with the chair drawn, making sure not to laugh at this display of chivalry. Veenu was quite pleased with his chivalry actually. He had a big smile as he took his seat.

Now that they were both comfortably seated, Veenu looked at Vini. "Um" he said.

Vini's eyes really were beautiful.

"Yes" said Vini.

"Um" said Veenu. Vini's eyes mesmerized him.

"So" said Vini taking over. "I wonder what the *'personal'* reasons were that caused our founders to part ways?" She drew inverted commas in the air as she said the word 'personal'.

"Yes" said Veenu. "The reasons were extremely 'personal'. Dr Suresh Sharma committed suicide!" He mimicked Vini's inverted comma gesture as he said 'personal'.

"Suicide?" Vini's beautiful wide eyes widened further.

Veenu nodded. "After that there was no choice for the founders but to part ways" he said.

"How did you know?" asked Vini impressed.

"I did some research on the net as soon as I got to our guest house. He was found hanging by a rope from the ceiling of his apartment."

"Wow" said Vini. There was a slight pause as the information sank in. "But why?"

"Apparently his girlfriend left him" said Veenu. "She did not feel secure being with a security expert!"

The hostess was back with the drinks menu and handed one each to Vini and Veenu. They both opened them directly in front of their faces.

"Some wine?" asked Veenu peeping over the top of his menu.

"I would love some" said Vini. Her beautiful eyes peeped over the top of her menu. "Which one would you recommend?"

Veenu's face disappeared behind his menu. "How about this one?" he said.

"Sure" said Vini staring at the back of Veenu's menu. "I trust your choice."

"Done" said Veenu emerging from behind his menu.

The hostess magically re-appeared at their side as soon as Veenu put his menu down. "Ready to order some drinks, sir" she asked?

"Rose" said Veenu. He took the single long stemmed red rose from the vase in the center of the table and held it out for Vini.

"Thank you" said a surprised Vini with genuine pleasure. She accepted the rose and kept it next to her dinner knife.

"Ready to order some drinks sir?" repeated the hostess.

"Yes. A glass of Merlot for the beautiful lady" said Veenu nodding towards Vini, "and a coke for me."

If the hostess was surprised at this somewhat strange order, she did not show it. "Very good sir. Anything else?" she said.

"No. That's all."

The hostess left. Vini was looking incredulously at Veenu.

"A coke?!" said Vini. She seemed slightly peeved. "You are making me have a wine while you are having a coke?"

"Oh" said Veenu. "You can share some of my coke if you like."

It seems that the beautiful hostess with the fixed smile was meant only to enhance the initial restaurant experience and create a good first impression for they were served their drinks by an expressionless, stout male waiter wearing a tight black suit, stitched for someone with a much smaller stomach.

"Cheers" said Veenu loudly picking up his large coke glass.

"Cheers" repeated Vini holding up her much more delicate looking wine glass.

The glasses 'clinked' as they were tilted forwards.

Behind the clinking glasses the hostess was seating someone that looked like a typical Bangalore software engineer. Now, in this city a software engineer is a very broad species whose specimens vary a great deal in their appearance dress and even personality. Indeed just about any adult human being you are likely to run into or spot from the distance, in the malls, at the cinema, in a restaurant, in one of the many pubs, in the streets or anywhere else in this unique city is more likely to be a software engineer than anything else. Even your scuba diving instructor if you happen to take a scuba diving class over the weekend and the long haired guitar player in a live band are most likely just moonlighting from their day jobs as software engineers.

So irrespective of appearance, it would have been reasonably safe to assume that the man now being seated behind the cheering glasses was a software engineer but this particular specimen looked more like a Bangalore software engineer than anybody else at the restaurant. He was about 5 feet 7 inches tall, somewhat dark complexioned with non distinctive features, wearing a fully zipped up brown jacket (even though while pleasant, it was not really cold), dark pants and dull black leather shoes that looked like they had never been polished. A black motorcycle helmet still on his head completed the attire. His brow was furrowed and he seemed lost in thought. He was probably still thinking about why, despite his best efforts at debugging, his program continued to crash at startup. Nothing will get a software engineer's brow to furrow faster than a program that crashes at startup. I mean after all the long hours they put into coding it, the least they can expect a decently well behaved program to do is to *start up*! They do not mind so much if the program crashes when someone clicks on the menu item that is supposed to create a summary report of the profitability of a specified subsidiary but this persistent behavior of crashing even before the main window comes up really gets them down.

The Software Engineer sat down on the chair that the hostess had pulled out for him. He kept his jacket on, still fully zipped up but removed his helmet and attempted to keep it on the plate opposite his. The hostess moved quickly and deftly removed the plate from under the helmet just as it was about to come to rest on it. The helmet landed on the table cloth where the plate had been just moments ago, in between the knife and fork. The Software Engineer was not too bothered. It seems that he did not really mind keeping his helmet on the table cloth instead of the plate as originally intended. The expression on his face did not change from the brooding thoughtful look that he had entered with. The removal of the helmet had revealed a head with short cropped hair. The hair were short enough that they required no combing. The Software Engineer had probably shaved that morning but with a razor that was at least two months old. He had an uneven stubble.

The hostess tried to hand over the drinks menu to the Software Engineer.

"A large vodka with lime" he said without looking at it. He obviously wanted to drown his sorrows.

Veenu emerged from behind his dinner menu. "Ready to order?" he asked.

"Kung Pao Chicken for me please" said Vini.

Veenu decided to call the stout waiter so he could take their order. He was standing next to the hostess' desk near the entrance staring thoughtfully at the wall in front of him. Veenu stared at the waiter with his most piercing glance. But the waiter was studying the wall and did not notice. Veenu raised one hand and waved. "Hey" he said. The waiter continued to study the contours of the wall. Veenu raised both his hands above his head and waved frantically. "Yoo hoo" he shouted. The waiter shifted his weight from one foot to another. "Yoo hooo" Veenu shouted again.

"Don't make a spectacle of yourself" said Vini.

Veenu stopped waving his hands. "*You* call him" he said firmly.

Vini turned her head slowly towards the waiter who was behind her. As if it were drawn by a magnet, the stout waiter's head turned simultaneously towards Vini. Their eyes met. Vini blinked.

The stout waiter rushed towards Vini and Veenu's table as fast as his large stomach stuffed into the tight suit allowed him to looking quite comical in his haste.

"Your order sir" he said slightly out of breath looking at Veenu, pad and pencil in hand.

Veenu scowled at the waiter. Suddenly he gave a start, jumped off his seat and crouched behind it on the side away from the waiter. He slowly raised his head from under chair level until his eyes were peeping from just above the seat. He seemed to be staring at the stout waiter's legs which were at eye level in Veenu's current position.

"Your order sir" repeated the stout waiter looking down at Veenu.

Veenu's eyes moved up past the stout waiter's stomach to meet his.

"Kung Pao Chicken, American Chop Suey and Vegetable Chow Mein" said Veenu.

The stout waiter noted this down in his pad. "Very good sir" he said.

The stout waiter's departure revealed the reason for Veenu's strange behavior. The Lava Crater Head Man was seated on the table which would have been visible through the stout waiter's legs in Veenu's crouching position.

"Sit on your chair" instructed Vini.

Veenu sat on his chair but shielded the right side of his face with his right hand in the hope that this would prevent the Lava Crater Head Man from recognizing him.

"Do you always jump off your chair when you order your food?" asked Vini not sure of her partner's habits. This was the first time she was having dinner with him.

"No. No." Veenu shook his head. "It's that man." He pointed to the Lava Crater Head Man with a slightly raised finger of the left hand. His right hand was still shielding his face.

Vini turned her head to look at the Lava Crater Head Man. "What a strange looking man" she said. Of course the Lava Crater Head Man did look somewhat comical with his reddish, round face topped with reddish, orange hair pointing straight upwards, fairly long at the edges but progressively shortening in length until they reached the bald patch in the center. A tomato seed was still stuck on his nose and another one on his forehead. "But why are you scared of him? Is he a friend of yours?"

"I am sure he is plotting to throw tomato juice on me" said Veenu.

Vini burst out laughing. (What a nice laugh she had.) "Why would he want to throw tomato juice on you?" she asked.

Veenu told her that morning's story of how he had managed to send a stream of seed laden tomato juice hurtling towards the Lava Crater Head Man which had hit him in a straight line starting from his forehead and going over his nose and lips down to the top of his tie, and how the Lava Crater Head Man had spread the juice all over his face with the plastic covered paper tissue.

Vini laughed and laughed. She turned to look at the Lava Crater Head Man more closely. Those small spots on his forehead and nose and another one on the knot of his tie did look like tomato seeds!

"Even so" she said looking back at Veenu. "I am sure it's just a coincidence that he is here. I don't think he wants to throw tomato juice on you."

Veenu still looked unsure.

"You can bring your hand down" said Vini.

Veenu slowly brought his right hand, which was still shielding his face down to the table.

"Good" said Vini encouragingly.

Just then the stout waiter appeared at the Lava Crater Head Man's table. "Your tomato juice sir" he said loudly.

Vini and Veenu both turned to look at the Lava Crater Head Man. He had picked up his glass of tomato juice… and was sipping juice from it.

The man in the blue suit that Veenu had mistaken for a waiter was sitting behind Veenu, a little to the left of him.

He had not particularly enjoyed being mistaken for a waiter and kept looking at Veenu but looked away whenever Vini caught him looking. On Veenu's left the Software Engineer had been served his large vodka with lime. He was slowly sipping his drink. His expression was still as grave as before. Every now and then he stole glances at Veenu.

Veenu was still not sure that the Lava Crater Head Man had ordered tomato juice just so he could drink it and was keeping a wary eye on the glass. The Lava Crater Head Man also seemed to be looking towards Veenu. He too looked grave and had a furrowed brow.

"Why is he looking at me?" Veenu asked.

"*Everybody* is looking at you!" said Vini. She nodded her head first towards the man in the blue suit and then towards the Software Engineer. Veenu turned his head to look towards the man in the blue suit. Sure enough he had been looking at Veenu and quickly looked away when he saw Veenu turn his head. Veenu looked towards the Software Engineer. He too immediately looked the other way.

Veenu shook his head. "What a strange city" he said. "Here I am sitting with the most beautiful girl in the world and all the men in the restaurant are staring at … me! This would never happen in IIT."

"Thanks for the compliment" said Vini.

The service at this restaurant was fast. The stout waiter was serving them their food already.

"So" said Vini getting down to business once the waiter had left. "Do you have a girlfriend?"

"No." Veenu shook his head. He looked rather sad and puppy like.

"Never had one" he said after a slight pause.

"Never?" said Vini. "Not even in school?"

Veenu shook his head slowly and sadly. "I did like a girl in school" he said.

"Then what happened?" asked Vini with interest.

"Unfortunately her name turned out to be Priya" said Veenu.

Vini was perplexed. "Nothing wrong with that name" she said. Her fork full of food was poised halfway between the plate and her mouth.

"Yes. It's a nice name" agreed Veenu. "But I always used to call her Ritu so she never talked to me."

Vini dropped her fork on the plate. She was laughing loudly.

The *signature suspense tune* started again as Vini's laugh petered off. Vini and Veenu automatically turned to look at the Lava Crater Head Man. He was pointing his cell phone towards Veenu.

"What!?" Veenu exploded. "He is photographing me now?"

Veenu started to get up. Vini held his hand and restrained him. "Don't worry about it" she said. "He probably just likes you" she added with a twinkle in her eye.

Veenu sat down again. "I *don't* like his intentions" he declared.

Veenu turned his head to the other side. The Software Engineer immediately stopped looking at Veenu and took a big bite from his Chopsuey which had just arrived. Veenu turned back and glowered at Vini.

"Ignore him too" she said matter of factly. Unlike Veenu she was used to men staring at her in restaurants and quite adept at ignoring them.

The Lava Crater Head Man was not eating anything. He had kept his cell phone on his dinner plate, his fork was on one side of it and his knife and the empty glass of tomato juice on the other. It did not look like he intended to eat any of the wonderful food this restaurant was capable of serving. He was staring intently into his cell phone and typing something on it.

The *signature suspense tune* had started. Vini and Veenu automatically turned to look at the Lava Crater Head Man. The stout waiter had arrived at this table. "Your tomato juice, sir" he said keeping the fresh glass next to the empty one.

Veenu looked at the glass warily. The Lava Crater Head Man picked up the glass, looked towards Veenu again, brought the glass to his lips and took a big sip from it. The *signature suspense tune* stopped.

Vini and Veenu resumed eating. Veenu's style of eating was the same staccato style first seen on the plane. His fork would rest comfortably on the table while he chewed slowly or talked to Vini. Once done with his chewing, his hand would move slowly to pick up his fork, gather up some food and then suddenly move at high speed to transport it to his mouth. Then everything would slow down again as the fork was slowly kept back on the plate.

With this style of eating the man in the blue suit and the Software Engineer were done with their dinner much before Veenu was. The man in the suit left but the Software Engineer looked like he was still pondering over his software problem. He ordered another Vodka and lime.

The stout waiter was back at Vini and Veenu's table once Veenu finished his food. "Dessert?" he inquired.

"Dessert?" repeated Veenu looking at Vini?

"Not for me" said Vini. "I am watching my figure."

"I am watching it too" said Veenu looking her up and down.

"Stop it!" said Vini. "Why don't you have some?" she added.

"Um" said Veenu.

"Dessert" said Vini.

"Yes. You sure you don't want any?"

"Absolutely sure" said Vini.

Veenu ordered the gooey chocolate brownie with vanilla ice cream drenched in hot chocolate sauce.

"Sounds yummmmy" said Vini.

The Software Engineer was looking at Veenu again. Veenu looked back at him. Of course the Software Engineer turned away. Veenu continued to look at him this time. He looked depressed.

"Poor guy" said Veenu. "He looks like he is having trouble debugging his software."

"Why don't you go talk to him?" suggested Vini. "After all he is a fellow software engineer."

"Good idea" said Veenu.

The sudden appearance of Veenu at the Software Engineer's table unnerved him.

"Yo" said Veenu cheerily.

"Yo" replied the Software Engineer softly.

In the background, Veenu's dessert along with the bill was being delivered to his table. It looked yummy. A good sized gooey chocolate brownie sat on a creamy base drizzled with chocolate. A scoop of Vanilla ice cream was placed on the brownie, topped with crushed nuts. Generous amounts of hot dark chocolate sauce flowed down all sides of the ice cream and onto the brownie.

"How is it going" said Veenu to the Software Engineer loudly.

"Fine" said the Software Engineer. His tone implied that things were not fine at all. "Fine" he repeated.

"Rough day at work?" said Veenu.

The Software Engineer nodded.

"Let me guess" said Veenu. "Your program is crashing and cannot figure out why?"

The Software Engineer looked up at Veenu. "Yes!" he said. "How did you know?"

"From your expression" said Veenu. "I am also a software engineer."

"Oh" said the Software Engineer. "You are a software engineer?"

"Of course. Of course" said Veenu. "In this city, who isn't?"

"Which Company do you work for?" continued Veenu.

The Software Engineer did not answer immediately.

"Info Systems or Wipro?" said Veenu. He was on a roll.

"Info Systems" said the Software Engineer.

"I knew it" said Veenu. "Listen, I am staying at the Company guest house just down the road. You know the one with the green roof and the amazing bougainvillea? It is a lovely guest house. Let's keep in touch. Drop in sometime."

The Software Engineer nodded. He made a mental note to steer clear of all houses with green roofs. Luckily there were not too many of those in this city.

"Now you go home and go to sleep" instructed Veenu. "Your problem will be solved by morning."

The Software Engineer smiled. He was quite amused by this proclamation.

"The same thing happens to me" continued Veenu. "Whenever I have a problem, I go to sleep!"

The Software Engineer smiled wider. "You go to sleep when you have a problem?"

"Yes" said Veenu. "By the time I wake up my problem has been solved by my sub conscious mind. I have a very powerful sub conscious mind." Veenu tapped the side of his head as he said this.

The Software Engineer tapped the side of his own head a couple of times. "He is mad" he thought.

"Thank you" he said aloud nodding. "Sub conscious mind. I will remember."

Veenu returned to his table quite pleased with himself at having cheered up the Software Engineer. He beamed at Vini. "You saw that?" he said. "I have solved his problem."

"I saw" said Vini.

"Now where's my dessert?" said Veenu sitting down. "I have earned it."

"There" said Vini pointing to a tiny little spoonful sized piece of gooey chocolate brownie sitting on top of a small amount of melted vanilla ice cream.

"That's it?!" exclaimed Veenu loudly.

"It was yummmy" said Vini licking her lips.

'You ate it all?" shouted Veenu.

"Not *all*" said Vini. "I left some for you."

She scooped up the leftover piece of gooey chocolate with one finger and brought it to Veenu's lips. Veenu opened his mouth and Vini's finger slipped inside. He sucked at the sinful chocolate as she pulled her finger out.

"How was it?" said Vini.

"Amazing" said Veenu.

Veenu stared longingly at the small amount of chocolate still stuck to Vini's finger as if he wanted more of it. But Vini put her finger into her own mouth and sucked of the remaining chocolate. Somehow Veenu did not feel like complaining.

"Bill" said Vini pointing to the leather folder that contained the bill.

"I will take that" said Veenu. He pulled the bill towards himself. He took the bill out its folder and gave it a dirty look but then pulled out a credit card and put it into the leather folder.

Vini looked toward the stout waiter and blinked. He rushed over to their table.

"All done? Can I take that" he said pointing at the table.

"Yes" said Veenu. He handed him the salt shaker.

The stout waiter accepted the salt shaker and stood staring at it, not sure what he was supposed to do with it.

"I think he wanted the payment" said Vini.

"Oh" said Veenu. This time he handed over the leather folder.

Vini and Veenu descended the stairs to the eclectic shop below. Vini stopped to browse. She was fascinated by the translucent candles with the real flower petal leaves encompassed within the wax. Veenu hung around beside her.

"While you are looking around here, could I just go over to the computer shop next door" he asked. "I will be back in five minutes."

"Ok" said Vini.

The *signature suspense tune* began as Veenu ran out leaving Vini alone in the shop.

It was dark outside. The computer shop was still open although it was getting late. It must have been past 10:00 PM. Veenu went inside.

Vini was inspecting one of the candles in the shop. A man was coming down the staircase. He was not visible yet but the light behind him cast his shadow on the staircase. The shadow grew longer as the man descended.

A cold breeze blew in through the open door. Vini shivered slightly. She looked around. There was nobody else in the shop. The shadow had stopped moving. Vini did not know why, but she felt a bit scared. She quickly gathered a couple of candles and a handmade green translucent soap and went over to the payment counter. There was nobody there. The shadow on the stairs moved slightly backwards.

"Hello" said Vini. There was no answer. A curtain behind the payment counter moved slightly in the breeze.

"Helloooo" repeated Vini.

A hand was placed on Vini's shoulder. The lights went out. Vini screamed loudly. The scream reverberated throughout the shop in the darkness.

Someone rushed out from behind the curtain. The sound of several running feet came from the staircase.

There was the sound of a generator starting up and the lights came back on. Vini's face was white. The payment counter lady was glaring at Vini from behind the counter looking concerned. The hostess, the stout waiter and the Software Engineer, his helmet back on his head were staring down from the staircase. The Lava Crater Head Man's head was visible behind them.

Vini turned her head to look behind her. It was Veenu! He had withdrawn his hand from her shoulder and was looking very sheepish.

"It's you?" said Vini relieved.

"Sorry" said Veenu embarrassed. "I did not mean to scare you."

The payment counter lady, the hostess, the stout waiter, the Software Engineer and the Lava Crater Head Man all stared at Veenu suspiciously while Vini paid for her purchases.

"Why did the lights go off?" asked Veenu nonchalantly.

"No electricity" said the payment counter lady coldly. "It happens. The generator takes a few seconds to start up."

Five pairs of eyes continued to stare at Veenu as Vini and Veenu left the shop together.

It had become quite cool outside. A cool breeze was coming in from the forested side of the road. The road did have street lights but there was no electricity and the lights had gone out. It was dark except for the light from the restaurant which was running on the generator and a bit of light from a few houses that had UPS. The sky had become cloudy. The moon was peeking in and out of the clouds. It became really dark when the moon hid behind a cloud but improved dramatically when the moon looked out. Long eerie shadows formed on the road from the dim light of bungalows with UPS.

The *signature suspense tune* had started again. Veenu took out his cell phone to throw a little light on the road as they walked along it. It started to drizzle. Vini was cold and was shivering slightly. She was still a little shaken up from her encounter in the shop and had to keep telling herself that it was just Veenu's hand that had made her scream. She moved closer to him. Her shoulder touched his as they walked.

Vini felt like they were being followed. She looked back. She saw the dark helmeted figure of the Software Engineer in the light of one of the houses but he was quite a bit behind them. It is just the poor software engineer on his way home she thought.

"I' m cold" she said aloud to Veenu. She pressed closer against him.

Veenu still had his cell phone in his left hand but he put his right arm around Vini's shoulder. Or rather, he started to put it around her shoulder but stopped just before his hand touched her. He was not sure if he should be doing this. His hand hovered over her shoulder. He lowered it slightly and one finger touched her shoulder momentarily but went up again.

Vini watched his hesitating hand hovering over her shoulder from the corner of her eyes. "IIT Idiot" ("*IIT Ka dhakkan*" in the Hindi translation) she muttered under her breath. She caught Veenu's hand with her own and pulled it down over her shoulder.

"What did you say?" asked Veenu. His arm now rested comfortably around her neck with his hand on her shoulder.

"Nothing" said Vini. She put her arm around Veenu's waist. She felt much warmer and safer now.

The moon had gone behind a thick cloud and it had become very dark. There was no light from any of the houses on this part of the road. There was a sound of running feet behind them. Alarmed, they both stopped and turned around to look behind them. Just a few feet behind them the helmeted figure of the Software Engineer was grappling with another man. A bolt of lightning lit up the figures for a split second and illuminated a gruesome scene. The Lava Crater Head Man had a knife in his hand. The knife was poised just above the Software Engineer's chest about to plunge in. Vini's scream mingled with that of the Software Engineer as the knife plunged into him in the darkness. The screams gave way to loud thunder. The Software Engineer fell back on to the road with a loud cracking sound as his helmet hit the road.

The moon had started to peek out from behind the cloud and it had become slightly less dark. The Lava Crater Head Man stood staring at Vini and Veenu. The knife was still in his hand and was dripping with fresh blood. They stood frozen staring back at the Lava Crater Head Man. Were they going to be next?

Veenu's first instinct was to run away but he looked down at the Software Engineer's still writhing body and found himself running towards the Lava Crater Head Man instead. The Lava Crater Head Man hesitated but then, in spite of the knife in his hand, he turned around and ran… away from Veenu. He disappeared into the darkness.

Veenu knelt beside the Software Engineer's body. The moon was fully out from behind the cloud. It illuminated the body. The Software Engineer's jacket was drenched with blood. He had stopped writhing and lay quite still. Veenu felt the Software Engineer's neck for a pulse.

Vini was standing next to Veenu now. "Is he…?"

There was another bolt of lightning. "He's dead" declared Veenu looking up towards Vini. "The Lava Crater Head Man has killed him." His words mingled with the thunder.

Chapter 5

The Police

It had started raining heavily. The rain was washing off the blood from the Software Engineer. Vini and Veenu had both become very wet. Veenu shielded his cell phone with his hand and shone the light on the Software Engineer's face. His eyes were still open. His face was frozen in a grotesque frightened scowl. Veenu closed the Software Engineer's eyes with his hand.

"Help me drag him to the side of the road" he said.

Vini and Veenu each grabbed one of the Software Engineer's legs and pulled the body towards the forested side of the road. The Software Engineer's helmeted head bounced slightly on the rough road as he was dragged to the side and brought to rest under a tree.

Vini took out her cell phone from her jean's pocket and called the police.

***

It had stopped raining and the street lights were back on. The wail of a siren announced the arrival of an ambulance closely followed by a police jeep. Soon the Software Engineer's body was moved into the ambulance.

The police inspector asked a few questions to Vini and Veenu. He noted their contact details and inspected their ids. "You will be required in the police station tomorrow" he said. He let them go.

They walked back to *the house with the green roof* in silence.

Just inside the main door, they stopped and looked into each other's eyes. Vini put her still wet arms around Veenu and gave him a hug. Her long hair, still wet pressed against his cheek.

"Bye" she said.

They walked to their own rooms on opposite sides of the main door.

It was almost midnight now. Veenu felt tired and sleepy but he needed to do a few more things before he could go to sleep. He sat at his desk in front of his Corn System's laptop, the bright yellow corn on the cob logo clearly visible on its back.

The *signature suspense tune* had begun.

A man's shadow appeared on the wall behind Veenu. The shadow grew bigger as the man moved noiselessly towards Veenu.

Veenu sensed someone's presence in the room. He turned around.

"Thank you" said the Japanese Gentleman.

"You?" exclaimed Veenu. "How did you get in?"

"Dool open" said the Japanese Gentleman. "So I come in."

This logic was not obvious to Veenu.

"To say thank you" added the Japanese Gentleman.

Veenu got up from his chair. "You are welcome" he said sounding irritated. He started to push the Japanese Gentleman out of his room.

"No. No" he protested. "You don't undelstand. That vely impoltant watch. I am in debt for life."

Veenu was alarmed. He managed to gently push the Japanese Gentleman out the room and quickly closed the door.

"And stay out" he said under his breath as he locked the door.

————◆————

The sun was streaming in through Veenu's window. Sun rays brightly illuminated his sleeping face. There was not a cloud in the sky. Last night's events seemed like a bad dream.

Veenu's cell phone rang. He scowled, his eyes still closed. The phone rang again insistently. He opened one eye and gave a one eyed dirty look to the phone lying next to his face. It had no effect on the phone which continued to ring.

He picked up the phone and balanced it on his ear, without moving his head from the pillow. His open eye closed again.

"Hello" he said sleepily.

"Mahalingam this side" a gruff voice growled into his ear.

"Maha who?"

"Lingam" said the gruff voice. "Maha Lingam."

"You are wanted in the police station imm-ee-diately."

"Police station?" repeated Veenu. He remembered the murder from last night and sat up suddenly. The phone slid of his ear, bounced on the pillow and clattered to the floor.

"Hallo" the gruff voice growled from the floor. "Hallo. Hallo."

Veenu leaned over the bed and picked up the phone.

"HALLO" Mahalingam shouted in his ear.

"Hallo" said Veenu. "I mean hello."

"Yes" said Mahalingam. "You are wanted in the police station imm-ee-diately."

'Why?" asked Veenu.

"Because of the murder" said Mahalingam surprised at the question.

"Oh god!" said Veenu. "I thought that was a dream."

"And get your girlfriend along with you" said Mahalingam.

"Girlfriend?"

"Yes. Miss… Misssss Vini" said Mahalingam reading out the name.

"She is not my girlfriend" said Veenu.

"Whatever she is, get her" growled Mahalingam. "The Chief Inspector wants her too."

"Yes sir. Mr. Mahalingam, sir" said Veenu.

"Come quickly" said Mahalingam a little less gruffly.

Veenu got out of bed. His was wearing a faded pink pyjama that did not quite manage to reach his ankles along with a faded pink kurta. He ran barefoot to Vini's room.

He knocked. There was no reply. "Was she still asleep?" He knocked again, this time loudly. He waited a bit but there was still no reply. "Where was Vini?" Veenu started banging on the door.

"Coming, coming" shouted Vini from behind the door. "Don't break the door."

The door opened about 3 inches. Vini peeked through the three inches with one eye.

"Oh" said Veenu. "You are in your room?"

"Of course I am in my room" said Vini. "You woke me up."

"Can I come in?" asked Veenu.

"No" said Vini.

That was not the answer Veenu was expecting. "Why not?" he said.

"Because I am not wearing any clothes" said Vini.

This revelation made Veenu forget what he needed to say. He opened his mouth and closed it.

"I don't wear clothes while sleeping" said Vini.

"Oh" said Veenu. There was a pause.

"You always wear pink pyjamas while sleeping?" asked Vini noticing Veenu's attire.

'I used to wear white pyjamas" said Veenu.

"Then? What happened?" said Vini not sure what Veenu was about to reveal.

"Then, one day I washed my clothes in my friend's washing machine" said Veenu.

Vini was still not sure where this was leading. What kind of a friend was this with whom Veenu shared his washing?

"Along with his red shirt" continued Veenu. "It leaked color and all my pyjamas became pink."

Vini laughed.

"They also shrank, I see" she said looking down at the space between the bottom of Veenu's pyjamas and his ankles.

Veenu nodded, sadly.

"Sooo?" said Vini. "Why did you wake me?"

"The Chief Inspector wants to see us" said Veenu remembering. "We have to go to the police station."

"imm-ee-diately" he added mimicking Mahalingam.

"Ok" said Vini. "I will take a quick shower and be in your room in ten."

"You can take a shower in my room" said Veenu suddenly.

"Why?" asked Vini surprised.

"Ummm" said Veenu.

Vini smiled. "I have my own bathroom" she said sweetly. "See you in ten." She closed the door.

Veenu stood staring at the door for a bit. He slowly started to walk back to his own room. Suddenly, he jumped and flattened himself against the wall. The Japanese Gentleman was prowling about in the dining area! He was looking dapper in a dark blue suit, shiny well polished black shoes and red tie. His slightly wet hair was neatly combed and flat against his head.

"Oh god" said Veenu to himself. "It's Thank You!"

He was probably waiting for Veenu to come out so he could thank him. "No?" He was headed towards the front door. "He is heading for his Maruti Esteem to go to work" thought Veenu. Veenu resumed his dangerous walk back to his room, this time on tip toes. He paused in the corridor just before he entered the dining area waiting for the Japanese Gentleman to exit. The Japanese Gentleman was turning the front door handle. But wait, he had paused and was thinking hard. Had he forgotten something? He turned around. He smiled. He had seen Veenu!

He ran towards Veenu. Veenu ran towards the dining table. The Japanese Gentleman ran after him. They ran round and round the dining table, the Japanese Gentleman in his dapper suit and shiny black shoes and Veenu barefoot in his short pink pyjamas. The Japanese Gentleman caught hold of a chair and stopped. Veenu ran a couple more steps before he realized that the Japanese Gentleman was now running in the opposite direction. Veenu too reversed directions with the help of a chair. But the Japanese Gentleman was much closer now. As Veenu approached a corner of the table he accelerated and veered off into his own corridor. The Japanese Gentleman followed but Veenu managed to enter his room and quickly shut the door just before he caught up. The poor Japanese Gentleman was left stranded outside. Veenu heaved a sigh of relief as he caught his breath back.

<hr>

Vini and Veenu arrived at the police station in an auto. A pot bellied police man was sprawled on a wooden chair outside the door. He was just starting a yawn.

"Mahalingam?" said Veenu.

The police man completed his yawn and pointed to the door with his thumb.

Vini and Veenu walked inside.

"Mahalingam" said Veenu to the nearest pot bellied police man.

"Myself Ramalingam" said the policeman. "Yourself?"

"Myself Veenu" said Veenu. "I am here because of the murder."

"You have murdered someone" asked Ramalingam getting excited.

"No. No. Not me" said Veenu alarmed.

"She?" said Ramalingam conspiratorially coming closer to Veenu and nodding slightly in the direction of Vini.

"No. No" said Veenu. "Not her either."

"Then?" said Ramalingam disappointed.

"Then? I…" started Veenu. "We are here to see Mahalingam. He called us here."

"Wait here" said Ramalingam.

Vini and Veenu stood around. Ramalingam sauntered up to a closed door that had a sign that read "Chief Inspector". He knocked loudly and shouted "Maha-Lingam."

The door opened to reveal – Mahalingam. He was wearing a uniform that was at least one size too small. Even so, it was difficult to tell whether his name was justified but he certainly had a maha belly. This belly was bigger than any that they had seen so far. It protruded far beyond the tight belt that Mahalingam was wearing.

Ramalingam said something to Mahalingam. The latter nodded and beckoned to Vini and Veenu. "Come" he said.

Mahalingam stood sideways in the Chief Inspector's door and gestured to Veenu to go in. Given the size of Mahalingam's belly there was hardly any space left for Veenu to go in. Veenu considered his options. He decided to squeeze in sideways past Mahalingam's belly. Even though he was going in sideways, Mahalingam's belly had to be compressed to allow him to squeeze in.

Vini was not going to squeeze past the belly. "You first" she said and followed Mahalingam into the Chief Inspector's room. They had entered a large room. The Chief Inspector was sitting behind a large wooden desk with a large flat screen computer monitor on it. Given the progressively increasing belly sizes that they had seen so far today, Veenu was expecting a man with the largest belly ever but he was disappointed. The Chief Inspector did not have a belly at all. He had a muscular, mean looking body. However he looked harassed. He had a thick crop of hair. Two tufts of hair stood out from both sides of his head at a forty five degrees angle. The harassed face along with the tufts of hair standing out from his head on either side, somewhat nullified the effect of the mean looking body.

Vini and Veenu were ushered into two wooden chairs on the opposite side of the desk and sat facing the Chief Inspector. Mahalingam went and stood next to the Chief Inspector. His stomach rested rather comfortably on the desk. He picked up a notepad and pencil from the desk. The Chief Inspector pushed the computer monitor and keyboard to one side from in front of his face. He had his own notepad and pencil in front of him. They were ready for the interrogation.

"Name?" said the Chief Inspector staring into his notepad.

"Veenu" said Veenu.

"Name?" said the Chief Inspector again.

"Veenu" said Veenu.

The Chief Inspector looked up. He scowled at Veenu. "Your name" he said pointing at Vini.

"Vini" said Vini.

The Chief Inspector looked back into his notepad. "Address?" he said.

"No B 79, Koramangala, 9th Block, 2nd Cross, Bangalore, India" said Veenu. There was a pause as the Chief Inspector wrote this down. He looked up from his notepad into Veenu's eyes.

"It is a beautiful house with the green roof" said Veenu helpfully.

The Chief Inspector scowled. "Answer only when asked" he said.

"Yes sir" said Veenu.

"What do you do?" said the Chief Inspector.

"I am a software engineer" said Veenu.

"Which Company?"

"Corn Systems."

"What?"

"Corn. Corn. C-o-r-n Systems" Veenu spelt it out while trying to draw the outline of a corn on the cob in the air with his fingers.

The Chief Inspector scowled. "How long have you been working there?"

Veenu considered. "Zero days" he said.

The Chief Inspector stared dirtily at Veenu. "Don't make a fool of me" he said. "You software engineers think that the Bangalore police are a bunch of fools. Do you? Do you work for this… this" he consulted his notes. "Corn" he continued scornfully "Systems or not?"

"Yes sir" said Veenu. "I mean no sir."

The Chief Inspector dropped his pencil forcefully on the table and gave Veenu his dirtiest look so far. "Yes or no?" he shouted. "Mahalingam!"

On this cue, Mahalingam scowled at Veenu. "Answer properly" he said.

"No sir" said Veenu. "I used to work there but I… I got fired. I am not working anywhere now."

"Not working" repeated the Chief Inspector and wrote something in his notepad. "How long did you work at this, this Corn Systems before you got fired?"

Veenu considered his answer carefully. "Zero days" he said.

The Chief Inspector scowled his biggest scowl so far. "Mahalingam!" he growled.

"Answer properly" Mahalingam bellowed.

"Did you work for this Corn Systems or not?" asked the Chief Inspector sternly.

"Yes sir" said Veenu. "I mean no sir. I got fired before I joined."

The Chief Inspector stared at Veenu for a while. "Where did you work before you did not join Corn Systems?" he said finally.

"Nowhere" said Veenu.

The Chief Inspector stared harder.

"I was studying at IIT. IIT Delhi sir. I just came to Bangalore yesterday." Veenu explained

"First day. Murder!" said the Chief Inspector softly, shaking his head.

'And this girl?" said the Chief Inspector pointing at Vini but looking at Veenu. "Your girlfriend?"

"No. No" said Veenu vehemently. "She is not my girlfriend."

"Then what is she?" said the Chief Inspector. "Your wife?"

"No. No No." Veenu laughed. "She is… she is just my friend."

"Just your friend" said he Chief Inspector scornfully. He turned to Vini. "Address?" he said.

"No B 79, Koramangala, 9th Block, 2nd Cross, Bangalore" said Vini.

The Chief Inspector's brow furrowed. He seemed to be deep in thought. "Where have I heard that address before?" he said to himself softly. He looked at the ceiling.

"Just now" said Veenu helpfully. "From me."

The Chief Inspector looked at his notes. "Yes!" he said. He turned towards Vini. "This joker stays with you?" he asked.

"He is not a joker" she said firmly.

The Chief Inspector scowled at her. "This is my police station" he said. "If I say he is a joker then he *is* a joker."

"Mahalingam" he barked. "Is this fellow a joker or not?"

"I am not sure sir" said Mahalingam. "I will investigate." He wrote something in his notepad.

The Chief Inspector scowled at Mahalingam. He turned back towards Vini. "Do you stay with this jo.. fellow? He asked.

"No" said Vini. "It is not like that."

"You stay at B-79, Koramangala?" asked the Chief Inspector.

"Yes" said Vini.

"Which floor?"

"Ground floor" said Vini.

"And you stay at B-79 Koramangala" said the Chief Inspector turning towards Veenu.

"Yes sir" said Veenu.

"On which floor?"

"On the ground floor" said Veenu.

"Then you stay together in the same house on the same floor" concluded the Chief Inspector triumphantly.

"Yes, but I don't stay with him." Vini was quite firm about it.

The Chief Inspector gave Vini one of his choicest dirty looks. "You think that the Bangalore police consist of a bunch of fools?" he shouted. He wagged his finger in Vini's face. "I want straight answers from now on."

"Mahalingam" he thundered.

Mahalingam scowled at Vini. "Answer properly" he growled.

The Chief Inspector considered himself to be a patient man but just getting basic information such as name and address from these two buffoons was proving to be a challenge. The Chief Inspector's blood pressure was rising. The doctor had advised him to stay calm. "Calm down" he said to himself under his breath. He closed his eyes and took a few deep breaths. He felt better now. He was ready to proceed.

"Housewife or working?" he asked Vini.

"Working" she replied.

"Where?"

"Corn systems" said Vini.

The Chief Inspector stared at Vini. Dare he ask her for how long?

"But I too got fired before I joined" said Vini quickly. She smiled sweetly.

The Chief Inspector scowled at her. This was not getting anywhere. He decided to skip the preliminaries and get to the point. He forced himself to smile at Veenu. "Ok. Tell me" he said. "What did you see yesterday?"

"Not much" said Veenu. "I got here yesterday and did not get time to see anything. Of course I did see the airport.

Nice airport you have here. And I saw whatever I could from the car on the way to ITPL. It was a nice drive. Bangalore is a beautiful city. I saw some beautiful flowering trees along the way in Cubbon Park. The trees were fully covered with purple flowers with no leaves at all. Quite amazing actually. And then later I looked around a bit at ITPL. Amazing! Different kind of amazing than the trees of course. I was impressed by…"

Veenu stopped in mid sentence because he noticed that the Chief Inspector had put his head down on the table, his chin pressing against it. He had caught hold of the tufts of hair that were sticking out from both sides of his head and was pulling hard, as if he was trying to pull out his hair.

Veenu smiled. "Ah. That explains why his hair sticks out like that" he thought.

"Stop. Stop. Stop" shouted the Chief Inspector. He raised his head from the table. "In the night? What did you see in the night?"

"Oh? In the night?" said Veenu. "Vini took me to this really nice rooftop restaurant with this really interesting shop on the ground floor. Vini liked the translucent candles with the real flower petals encased in the wax. I wondered what happens to those petals when the candle burns. I think the petals might be catching fire causing the flame to change colors in interesting ways from time to time…"

"Stop!" The Chief Inspector's head was back on the table and he was pulling his hair out even harder than before.

Veenu stopped. He thought he had been doing a good job of describing the candles. He looked quizzically at the Chief Inspector.

"Don't make a fool of me" said the Chief Inspector in a low sinister voice. "I am *not* interested in candles. Tell me about the *murder*."

"Yes" said Veenu. "It was gruesome. The Lava Crater Head Man killed the Software Engineer with a knife."

"The who?" asked the Chief Inspector.

"The Lava Crater Head Man" said Veenu. "That is not his real name. In fact I don't even know his real name but he has reddish orange hair which sticks out straight up from his head at ninety degrees.

"Sort of like yours" continue Veenu pointing at the Chief Inspector's hair "except that yours is at about a forty five degrees angle to the ground… and not all of it sticks out, only a tuft of it on either side. I would say that the Lava Crater Head Man's hair is funnier looking. His head looks like it is a lava crater with the hair all around it progressively getting shorter and disappearing completely into the bald spot in the center… which is where you would expect the lava to start flowing from, if it were a real lava crater and not someone's head.

Veenu was quite pleased at having done such a good job of describing the murderer but for some reason the Chief Inspector did not look pleased at all. His face looked pained.

With utmost control the Chief Inspector managed to keep his head off the table and asked "How do you know that this… this lava man is the killer?"

"I saw him doing it" said Veenu. "He plunged his knife into the Software Engineer's heart. It was horrible."

Vini shuddered as she remembered the sight. "Yes" she nodded. "It was really horrible. There was a lightning bolt just as the knife went in. So the whole scene was clearly visible. I wish I had not seen it."

There was silence for a few seconds as the Chief Inspector digested this information. "Why do you think this, uh lava man wanted to kill the Software Engineer?"

Veenu thought for a few seconds. "He did not" he said finally.

"No?" said the Chief Inspector surprised.

"No" said Veenu shaking his head. "He wanted to kill *me*!"

The Chief Inspector scowled. He looked doubtful. What was this new twist?

"He followed me from the restaurant" continue Veenu. "He ran towards me with a knife. The brave Software Engineer saw the Lava Crater Head Man running towards me with the knife. He intervened and ended up being killed."

There was another pause. "Ok. So why did he want to kill you?" asked the Chief Inspector.

"It was because of the tomato juice" said Veenu.

"Tomato juice?" said the Chief Inspector wondering if he had heard right.

"I squirted the Lava Crater Head Man with tomato juice in the morning" said Veenu. He seemed quite proud at having drenched the cold blooded murderer with tomato juice. "It went from here" Veenu drew a line with his finger from the top of his forehead, over his nose and down to his collar button "to here."

The Chief Inspector was sure he was going mad. He looked at Vini for support.

"Yes" said Vini nodding. "The tomato seeds were still stuck to his face."

The Chief Inspector scowled at her. He thought for a bit. "You squirted the lava man with tomato juice in the morning?" The Chief Inspector winced as he said this. He could not believe he was actually saying those words. "So both of you know this lava man from before?"

"He is not the lava man" Veenu clarified. "He is the Lava Crater Head Man."

'Whatever he is" yelled the Chief Inspector banging his fists on the table. "How do you know him?"

Veenu considered. "I don't really know him" he said. "I met him on the plane. He was sitting next to me and staring into my food. Then he was there at ITPL also." Veenu had just realized something. "He probably followed me there! And then he followed me to the restaurant. He kept staring at me there also."

"*All* the men in the restaurant were staring at Veenu" said Vini teasingly.

"Yes" said Veenu nodding. "Very strange men you have in Bangalore."

The Chief Inspector's head was on the table again. He was pulling his hair hard. Veenu was concerned. He was afraid that tufts of the Chief Inspector's hair would come out in his hands at any moment. He lowered his head so it was nearer to the Chief Inspector's head. "The Lava Crater Head Man drank up three glasses of tomato juice" he said.

The Chief Inspector took a deep breath. He decided to keep going. "Why did you squirt the lava man with tomato juice?" he said not bothering to raise he head from the table.

"It was not my fault" said Veenu. "The plane people gave me this strange looking round, red thing. I put my fork into it and it squirted the Lava Crater Head Man. If he had not been staring into my food so intently it would not have happened."

The Chief Inspector sat up slowly. His face was purple. "I don't believe any of this cock and bull story" he said in an ominous voice. "You think the Bangalore police consist of fools? You think you can come here from Delhi, go around killing the local people and then get away by making up a fantastic story about Corn Systems, red colored lava men and" his voice shook "and tomato juice?"

"No" shouted the Chief Inspector venomously pointing a finger at Veenu. "*You* are the prime suspect in this case."

"But" Vini protested.

"Quiet" bellowed the Chief Inspector turning to look at Vini. "*Both* of you are the prime suspects in this case." He paused. "Lava man" he said sarcastically. "Ha! If this lava man really exists, can you draw a picture of him?" He pushed his notebook towards Veenu.

"I will try" said Veenu a bit shaken. He picked up a pencil. He was not at all good at drawing but he did not feel like telling the Chief Inspector that. He drew a face as a child might. He drew two small dots for the eyes with a curved line on top of each for the eyebrows. He added smiling lips and a curved nose. Veenu stared at his work of art. Something was missing. Yes, he attached two semi circles to the sides for the ears. And now for the hair. The hair was important. Veenu drew several vertical lines emanating from the top of the head. He drew a dashed semi circle to try and show the slanting crater behind. Veenu ended by putting in a couple of dots on the forehead and another two dots on the nose. The finished picture looked like this:

Veenu pushed the notepad towards the Chief Inspector. The Chief Inspector stared at the picture. "What are these dots?" he finally asked pointing to the dots on the forehead and the nose.

"Those are the tomato seeds" said Veenu.

The Chief Inspector thumped his fist on the table. "You think I am a complete fool?" he shouted. "Mahalingam, take the ID copy and fingerprints of these buffoons."

The Chief Inspector got up from his seat. He looked down at Vini and Veenu and wagged his finger at them. "I am not arresting you" he paused "yet" he said. "But I am warning you. Do not try to run away. We will be watching you. As soon as the murder weapon is found, we will find your fingerprints on it and you will both be in jail forever." The Chief Inspector brightened up at this pleasant thought. "Ha ha ha" he laughed.

Vini and Veenu were fingerprinted and their driving licenses photocopied. They left the police station looking quite grave. The policeman on the chair outside the main door to the police station yawned as they left.

———◆———

Mahalingam had just entered the Chief Inspector's office. "We have a match for the dead man's fingerprints" he said. "We have a positive ID."

The Chief Inspector was excited. "Bring him up on my screen" he said.

Mahalingam walked up to the Chief Inspector's side of the desk, rested his stomach on the desk and typed something on the keyboard. The front and side profile of a man appeared on the screen with some text next to it. The face looked somewhat similar to that of the Software Engineer but the man on the screen had much longer hair and was well shaven.

The Chief Inspector pulled the screen towards himself. His eyes widened. He scrolled through the data on the right side of the faces. "Mahalingam" he said.

"Yes sir"

"I want you to find out everything you can about Mr. Veenu and his girlfriend."

"She is not his girlfriend sir" said Mahalingam.

The Chief Inspector put his head on the desk and pulled at his hair. Mahalingam waited patiently. The Chief Inspector eventually raised his head. The clumps on both sides of his head were sticking out straighter than ever.

"Whatever she is" he yelled. "Find out everything about them."

"Yes sir" said Mahalingam writing diligently in his notepad.

"And about this… this *Corn* Systems" continued the Chief Inspector saying the word 'Corn' with scorn.

"Yes sir"

"And" continued the Chief Inspector. "Track down the lava man. He was sitting next to Mr. Veenu on yesterday morning's flight from Delhi."

The Chief Inspector tore off the page from his notepad where Veenu had drawn his masterpiece. "Apparently he looks like this" he said handing over the drawing to Mahalingam.

"Yes sir" said Mahalingam.

———◈———

Vini and Veenu got off the auto and entered *the house with the green roof*, still looking a little grave because of the dire warnings of the Chief Inspector.

"I am so happy to be back home" declared Vini cheering up a little as she entered. "I know this is just a guest house but there is a certain warmth about this place. It feels like home to me."

Veenu nodded. It did feel like home after the session at the police station.

"Now, if you don't mind" continued Vini, I am going to take a hot shower and then take a nap. You interrupted my beauty sleep this morning."

"About that beauty sleep" said Veenu.

"Yes?" said Vini wondering what Veenu was going to say.

"It is working!" said Veenu.

"Thank you!" said Vini pleased.

"But I thought you already showered in the morning?" said Veenu.

"With you going 'imm-e-diately" in Mahalingam's tone, I did not get the time to take a proper shower" said Vini.

"Why don't you take a shower in my room?" Veenu suggested.

Vini was bewildered. "No. Thank you. I have a perfectly good shower in my own room.

"Cheers" Vini waved to Veenu and went off towards her room. Veenu stood looking at her walk back for a bit then sighed and walked in the opposite direction towards his own room. Vini gave a quick glance over her shoulder but Veenu had already turned around and did not see it.

It was night time and quite dark outside. Veenu was sitting at the dining table of *the house with the green roof* alone, looking downcast. The dining room windows were open. It was cloudy again tonight. The overcast night sky was visible through the open windows.

Vini walked in looking radiant. "Hi" she said to Veenu sweetly.

Veenu took some time to recover from her sudden appearance and the sweetness of the 'Hi'.

"Hi" he said finally. "I did not see you at lunch."

"I slept through it" said Vini. "I was mentally exhausted after the grilling at the police station, and the hot shower put me to sleep. I did not want any lunch anyway."

"So you did take a shower?"

"Of course I did" said Vini. "I was dying to get out of my clothes and into that hot shower."

There was a pause.

"The afternoon beauty sleep has done wonders" said Veenu.

"You mean I looked horrible in the morning?" said Vini in a hurt tone.

"No. No. I mean…" Veenu looked confused. He was not sure what he meant.

Vini laughed. Her eyes twinkled. She had a beautiful laugh. She pulled up a chair and sat down close to Veenu.

It started to pour outside. Vini shivered as a cold breeze blew in through the open window. "Oh the rain and the cold breeze, it reminds me of the murder yesterday" she said.

As if on cue there was a huge bolt of lightning that lit up the rain outside. Vini's face looked scared in the bright light from the lightning bolt. A huge clap of thunder followed the lightning. Vini jumped and clutched Veenu's hand.

Veenu looked a Vini's hand in his. "Where is the Japanese Gentleman" he said.

"Oh, he usually comes in late" said Vini. "I think he has dinner at work." She moved closer to him.

The camera moved away from Vini and Veenu, into the pouring rain outside. The sound of the rain became louder.

Veenu was back in his room. He was sitting in front of his desk, his Corn Systems laptop open in front of him. He was checking his email. "Could it be? Did he have an interview call already?" Yes, he did! He had a call from that iconic company, Info Systems, for tomorrow morning.

"Yes!" said Veenu pumping the air with his fist. He smiled at the pouring rain outside visible through his window. A lightning bolt streaked across the sky. The *signature suspense tune* started mingled with the rolling thunder that followed. Veenu closed his eyes. The image of the Lava Crater Head Man holding the knife in front of the Software Engineer's chest, about to plunge it in appeared before his eyes. He opened his eyes with a start. It was almost exactly 24 hours since the Software Engineer had been killed. The night appeared to be exactly the same as yesterday. Was the Lava Crater Head Man on the prowl again tonight?

Someone was knocking on Veenu's door. "Oh god! The Japanese Gentleman must be back from work" thought Veenu. "Probably best to just hear him out. Perhaps then he will stop hounding me."

"Who is it?" shouted Veenu moving towards the door.

His question was answered only by another insistent knock on the door. Veenu opened the door. The figure at the door lunged forward and put their arms around Veenu holding him in a tight embrace.

"Vini!" said Veenu.

Vini was excited. "I got an interview call!" she said releasing Veenu. She jumped up and down.

"Congratulations." Veenu smiled at her.

"So? What are *you* up to?" said Vini walking into Veenu's room without invitation. She was wearing tights and a loose T shirt.

Vini was staring at Veenu's laptop. Her voice broke into his thoughts. "*You* got an interview call too!" she said.

"Yes" said Veenu sheepishly.

Vini rushed towards him and hugged him again. "Congratulations!" she said.

This time Veenu was determined to hug her back and started to bring his arms up behind her. But before he could wrap them around her, she had broken off the hug.

She was staring into the rain now, a grave expression on her face.

"Do you know the *real* reason I came to your room?" she said looking directly at Veenu.

Veenu shook his head.

"Because I am scared" said Vini. "Every time I hear thunder the image of that poor Software Engineer being killed comes back to me."

Veenu nodded understandingly He had just seen that same image himself.

"So" declared Vini casually. "I have decided to sleep with you tonight."

Veenu opened his mouth to say something but no words came out. He opened it again. "Um" he began.

Vini interjected. "While you are standing there practicing your impersonation of a fish, I think I will take a hot shower." She disappeared into the bathroom.

Veenu stood there staring after her with his mouth still open for a second while his sharp IIT brain processed this information. This girl seemed to be fond of taking showers.

Then he moved much like the lightning flashing outside his window and jumped into the chair in front of his laptop. With slightly shaking hands he connected the USB cable lying on the desk next to his laptop into the laptop. The USB cable was going from his computer to the wall behind. It went up the wall and disappeared into it at the corner. Veenu double clicked on an icon on his desktop. The shower area of the bathroom came into clear focus on the computer screen!

A shapely hand holding a T shirt extended itself onto the computer screen and hung the T shirt on a hook on the wall opposite to the shower. The hand withdrew. It soon came into view again, this time holding a pair of tights and hung it on the same hook.

The shower faucet was not visible on the screen but a hand must have turned it for the shower started. The water was hot. Steam started to fill the bathroom. Vini moved into the shower. Only her silhouette was visible through the steam. Veenu watched transfixed as Vini danced to the music in the shower. She was obviously enjoying it.

All too soon, the shower was switched off. The music stopped. The outline of Vini's shapely body moved through the steam to pick up the tights and T shirt from the hook on the far wall and the she was gone from the screen. Veenu still sat staring at the empty steam filled screen. He heard the bathroom door being opening. Quick! He shut the lid of his laptop and turned his chair around to face Vini.

She was back in her tights and loose T shirt. She had not dried herself fully before wearing her clothes and the T shirt stuck to her body. Her long hair was still wet. She looked at Veenu suspiciously. Veenu looked embarrassed. He started whistling. Vini made a face at him. She shook her head vigorously. Water droplets flew all over the room. Some of them hit Veenu's face.

"Good night" said Vini moving towards the exit door.

"B..But I thought you were planning to sleep here tonight?"

"It stopped raining" said Vini pointing to the window. "I am not scared anymore."

Veenu looked out of the window. It had indeed stopped raining. The sky had cleared up. He could even see a few stars shining brightly.

"The Bangalore weather is sooo fickle" he said with feeling.

Vini smiled at him sweetly and was gone.

Veenu sat starting at the door for a while. He slowly turned back towards his computer. He opened the lid. The computer had gone into sleep mode when the lid was closed. It came out of sleep mode as Veenu opened the lid. Veenu hit Ctrl-Alt-Del and the login screen came up. He entered his password and was back to the video player. He hit the play button on it. The shower scene started playing again from the beginning.

Chapter 6

The Noose

The sun was streaming into Veenu's room. It illuminated an innocent and peaceful looking Veenu still in deep sleep. There was a knock on the door. The *signature suspense tune* had started.

There was another knock, this time a little louder. "Who is it?" Veenu mumbled.

Apparently this encouraged the knocker for Veenu's words were followed by a series of loud knocks. Veenu opened one eye but made no attempt to get up.

There was another loud knock. Veenu clutched his head. "Coming" he said loudly. He dragged himself out of bed. He was wearing his normal pink pyjamas which had ridden up to his knee on one of the legs and looked even shorter than usual. He slowly opened the door and groggily focused on the figure outside.

"You!!?"

It was the Japanese Gentleman, formally dressed in his dapper blue suit, red tie and pointy black shoes. He stood facing Veenu, who of course was barefoot in his short pink pyjamas, looking sleepy.

"Thank you" said the Japanese Gentleman. He started to come into the room.

Veenu winced. He held his head with one hand. "*Please* don't wake me up early in the morning by attempting to break down my door just to say thank you" he said in a peeved voice. He pushed at the Japanese Gentleman a little to get him away from there.

"But, but" he sputtered looking hurt.

"But what?" Veenu was not in a mood to appease the Japanese Gentleman. He was successful in pushing him enough so that he could close the door.

Veenu looked at the wall clock in his room as he walked back towards his bed. It was already 8:30. He had not intended to sleep for that long. He needed to hurry if he was going to make it in time for his interview with Info Systems. It would probably take him an hour to drive down to Electronic City at this time of the day. The Japanese Gentleman had done him a favor by waking him up. Veenu started to feel guilty for having yelled at him. It was not that early in the morning and if the Japanese Gentleman had not woken him up, he could well have been late for his important interview. And after all he was only trying to thank him. Veenu wondered why he had been trying to run away from him. Why didn't he just allow the Japanese Gentleman to say what he wanted to and then perhaps he would stop hounding him? In fact Veenu should be thanking the Japanese Gentleman for having woken him up this morning.

Immersed in these guilty thoughts, Veenu was quite happy when he heard another knock on the door. "Persistent bugger, that Japanese Gentleman" he thought. He smiled as he quickly opened the door.

"Hello" he started to say but there seemed to be nobody there. At least not at eye level. Veenu lowered his eyes. There was a short, mean looking, highly muscular bald guy standing there. The man was holding a noose made of thick white rope.

"Hello" he said looking up towards Veenu. Then in a swift movement he raised his arm and put the noose over Veenu's slightly lowered head, around his neck and started to pull. The rope was cutting into Veenu's neck and he could no longer breathe. He was being choked to death. He brought his hand up to the rope around his neck and pulled at it but it was too late. The rope was too tight around his neck for him to insert his fingers inside it. The short man was still tightening the noose around Veenu's neck. He had a grin on his face. He was enjoying it!

His eyes swam and his vision blurred. His face had become red. He felt as if his neck would break. He was losing consciousness…

Suddenly he felt the short man's heavy, bald head careen forward and hit him right in the chest. Veenu fell backwards with the force and landed on the floor of his room with a thud. The short man's body followed his and landed heavily on top of him.

What had happened was that the Japanese Gentleman had come rushing onto the scene and hit the short man with the full force of his body causing him to propel forward and hit Veenu. Veenu was hurt from the bald head hitting him in the chest and the heavy body landing on top of him, but the Japanese Gentleman's action had caused the short man to release the pressure on the rope and it had loosened slightly. Veenu tugged at the rope with both his hands and managed to slip his fingers between the rope and his neck. He took in a gasp of air. It hurt his neck to breathe in but at least he had some fresh oxygen in him.

But the assassin recovered quickly. He sat on Veenu's chest, which was also hurting badly from the impact of the assassin's bald head and resumed tightening the noose around Veenu's neck.

Through the corner of his blurry vision Veenu saw that the Japanese Gentleman had entered the room (uninvited as usual) and was trying to pull the assassin of his chest. But the assassin's pressure on the noose was working. Veenu lost consciousness.

In the meantime, the Japanese Gentleman unable to pull the assassin off Veenu's chest had taken to pummeling him on his bald head with his fists. Bang! He gave the assassin a hard box on his right ear with his clenched right fist. The assassin's head flew to the left. Bang! Even before the assassin's head had stopped moving, the Japanese Gentleman gave him another box, this time on his left ear with his left fist. The assassin's head reversed directions and flew off towards the right.

This was proving to be a major inconvenience for the assassin. He would have to take care of the Japanese Gentleman first and come back to the main task of continuing to tighten the noose around Veenu's neck later. In any case Veenu already looked like he was dead.

The Japanese Gentleman was bent down over the assassin, getting ready to box him on the (now rather red) right ear again. But with a sudden motion, the assassin stood up straight, aiming the center of his bald head at the Japanese Gentleman's chin. The head crashed into the chin at high speed. "Man, this guy has a hard head!" the Japanese Gentleman might have thought if he could think at all. As it is, the impact of the hard head on his square chin knocked all the thoughts out of his head. He tottered backwards and landed on his back on the bed with a loud thud followed by a creaking sound as the bed struggled to keep intact in spite of the heavy body falling on it. The Assassin flew into the air and landed on top of him. There was a loud crack as the bed gave way and broke into two. It was now in a sort of V shape with the Japanese Gentleman lying in the bottom of the V. The assassin sat on his chest. He put his hands around his neck and proceeded to indulge in his favorite past time – strangling people. No matter if he did not have a rope. He enjoyed it more with his bare hands anyway.

Veenu came to, to the sounds of gurgling noises from the Japanese Gentleman's throat. He still had the rope around his neck but without the pressure from the assassin's hands he could breathe a bit again. Something told Veenu that it was essential to get up quickly. He loosened the rope around his neck slightly and gulped in as much air as he could through his constricted throat. He got up unsteadily to see the horrible sight of the assassin intent at strangling the life out of the Japanese Gentleman.

Veenu grabbed the lamp from the pedestal next to the broken bed. The lamp had a hard translucent glass dome around the bulb. He raised the dome over the assassin's bald head. He brought it down. Hard. The assassin really did have a hard head. The glass dome cracked and broke into pieces over his head but did not seem to faze him much. He turned and looked menacingly at Veenu.

Veenu's hand had hit the switch on the lamp when he had swung it at the assassin so that the naked bulb now glowed brightly causing the assassin's bald head to shine in its glow. He swung the lamp again. The bulb cracked on the assassin's head. The prongs that hold the filament inside the bulb, lodged themselves into the skin of his head. Sparks flew as 220 volts of electricity surged through his head.

Aghast, Veenu pulled the lamp away. But it was too late. The assassin's shiny bald head had been charred black. He slumped forward and fell on top of the Japanese Gentleman, covering his face. Neither body on the bed was moving. Gingerly Veenu moved towards them. The bodies were lying in the valley of the broken bed. Veenu sat on the floor on his knees and knelt over to reach them. The rope dangled from Veenu's neck onto the assassin's back. He touched the assassin slightly on the shoulder and quickly withdrew his hand as if there was still an electric current in the assassin's body. He half expected the assassin to awaken at his touch and continue with his task of strangling all available people. But there was no movement. Veenu paused a bit and then felt the assassin's wrist for a pulse. There was none!

"Oh God!" said Veenu. "He is dead."

He grabbed the Japanese Gentleman's wrist. Was he dead too? There was no pulse. Veenu moved his fingers around the wrist desperate to find a pulse. This time his fingers were firmly on the vein. He felt it throb!

"Yesss" he shouted aloud. The Japanese Gentleman was alive, unconscious but alive.

Veenu put his hands around the assassin's shoulders and tried to lift him off the Japanese Gentleman. This guy was heavy! His body lifted slightly but Veenu could not sustain the lift in this awkward position and the assassin fell back on top of the Japanese Gentleman's face. "That heavy body must be crushing him" thought Veenu. How to get the assassin off and allow him to breathe freely? He was sure that the Japanese Gentleman needed more oxygen than he was getting.

Veenu loosened the noose around his neck and slipped if off his head. He expanded the noose further and put it over the assassin's charred head and all the way down to his shoulders. Then he went to the side of the bed, grabbed at the free end of the rope and pulled with all his strength. The noose tightened around the assassin's shoulders and chest. Slowly the assassin's torso lifted up, straightened out and fell on the other side with his face facing upwards.

Veenu rushed over to the other side of the bed and loosened the Japanese Gentleman's tie. He opened the collar button. He put his ear next to the Japanese Gentleman's nose. Yes, he could feel his breath. Thank god for that.

Veenu stood back and surveyed the scene in front of him. The Japanese Gentleman was still unconscious but seemed to be breathing peacefully now. The assassin's head was lying next to the Japanese Gentleman's pointy black shoes which were pointing towards the roof. His mouth was open. His bald head was charred and black.

"What do I do now?" thought Veenu.

He rushed over to Vini's room. He knocked urgently on the door.

"Coming" said Vini from inside.

"What's your hurry?" she said as she opened the door. She was dressed in a formal silk salwar suit looking lovely.

Veenu's mouth opened. He was not used to seeing Vini dressed up. "um" he said.

"Still practicing your impersonation of a fish, I see" said Vini. She looked down at his Pyjamas. "Do you intend to go for your interview dressed up in those silly pink Pyjamas that are two sizes too short?"

"No" said Veenu.

"Then you had better get ready quickly. Your interview is before mine and I am ready already."

"Yes but.."

"But what?"

"There is a dead man in my room!" said Veenu.

"What?!" said Vini. Veenu's face told her that he was serious. "How did a dead man get into your room?"

"He came in through the door" said Veenu.

Vini stared at him.

This was not going well. This was not the time for explanations anyway. "Come with me" said Veenu. The urgency was obvious in his voice.

They ran towards Veenu's room.

Vini gasped as she took in the scene in Veenu's room. A broken bed with the Japanese Gentleman lying in the valley of the bed, his head on one end and his pointy black shoes on the other. A blackened bald head on the Japanese Gentleman's feet just beyond the black shoes with an open mouth set in an ugly face, a thick white rope tied around the man's shoulder and dangling over the bed from in between two black shoes. Pieces of broken glass strewn all over the bed, the broken lamp on the pedestal next to the bed.

"Are they…?" said Vini. "Are they both dead?"

"No" said Veenu. "The Japanese Gentleman is alive. He seems to be unconscious. The assassin is dead."

Vini did not trust Veenu's prognosis. She rushed to the bed and put her hand around the assassin's neck to feel his pulse.

"Yes. He is dead" she confirmed.

"What happened here?" she asked looking at Veenu.

Veenu explained hurriedly as best as he could how the assassin had knocked on his door and tried to strangle him and how the Japanese Gentleman had saved him and how he had unintentionally electrocuted the assassin while trying to save the Japanese Gentleman.

"But what do we do now?" he asked.

Vini considered. "We both have important interviews to attend" she said finally "and there is nothing much that we can do here right now."

"Yes" agreed Veenu.

"The Japanese Gentleman will probably wake up in a few minutes" said Vini. "Let us just make him a little more comfortable."

They set about their task. Veenu put his arm under the Japanese Gentleman's shoulders and Vini grabbed his legs. Veenu pulled the shoulders towards the head of the bed while Vini pulled the legs towards the foot of the bed. Much heaving and pulling later they managed to position him nicely on the bed with his head resting comfortably on a pillow at the head of the bed, his body sloping down the broken bed. His bottom nestled comfortably in the bottom of the V and his legs sloped up from there and ended with the black leather shoes at the foot of the bed. The pointy shoes pointed straight up at the ceiling. There was a peaceful expression on the Japanese Gentleman's face and he was breathing evenly.

Veenu beamed at Vini, quite pleased at their handiwork. Then he shuddered as he glanced at the would be assassin lying bent over himself on the bed. His ugly face was contorted and mean looking. He scared Veenu even though Veenu knew that he was dead.

"What do we do about him" Veenu asked Vini lowering his voice to a whisper. He pointed delicately at the ugly figure.

"Well…" Vini considered. "We can't leave him like that. Let us make him to a little more comfortable on the bed as well."

So Veenu grabbed the assassin's shoulder and Vini his legs. They heaved and pulled as usual until the short but heavy fella was correctly positioned on the bed next to the Japanese Gentleman. His bottom rested at the bottom of the V, almost touching the Japanese Gentleman's bottom. The rest of him sloped up on either side of the V of the broken bed. The short assassin was much shorter than the Japanese Gentleman and his ugly head did not quite reach the head of the bed. Instead it lay next to the Japanese Gentleman's chest.

The assassin's black shoes were just a little less pointy than the Japanese Gentleman's. Both pairs of shoes were pointing towards the ceiling; it would have been quite a comical sight had we not been talking about a dead man and an unconscious one.

"Ok" said Vini satisfied. "Now we both have interviews to attend. There is no time to call the police or anything like that. Our taxies should be here already."

"Better get into some decent clothes at super fast speed" said Vini looking at the gap between Veenu's pink pyjamas and his ankles. "I am off."

Vini started moving towards the door. Then suddenly she stopped. She turned and ran towards Veenu. She gave him a quick hug and before he could bring his arms up to hug her back, she was off again.

"Wish me luck" she said looking back from the door.

"Good luck" Veenu managed to shout back just before she went out of the door.

Veenu stood staring at her. "I really must learn to hug quickly" he thought. He practiced bringing his arms up quickly from his sides and wrapping them around himself a couple of times. Something made him look towards the window. Vini was at the gate looking towards him. She waved goodbye to him. "Had she seen him practicing his hugs?" Veenu looked embarrassed as he waved back and watched her move out of view.

Veenu had just realized that he needed to get dressed for his interview. He started to move like lightening. He had a substantial stubble but there was no time to shave or to take a bath. A blur of movement later his pink pyjamas and kurta were lying in a heap on the floor and he was in a semi formal shirt and pants. His movements slowed to the point where you could actually see him as he sat on the bed beside the Japanese Gentleman to put on his white socks and the dirty 'used to be white' sneakers.

The *signature suspense tune* had started.

Flaming, pointing upwards hair appeared at the base of Veenu's window. The hair moved upwards. Soon the full, mean face of the Lava Crater Head Man was visible through the window. He was staring at Veenu. He must have taken a good bath since killing the Software Engineer because there was no sign of any tomato seeds on his face. His lava crater hair pointed upwards straighter than ever before.

Veenu froze in the act of tying his shoelace. He turned his head slowly towards the window. But there were no faces there. He could see that it was a beautiful sunny day outside.

Veenu shook his head. He resumed the task of tying his shoelaces and rushing for his interview. He turned at the door for a final look at the two bodies lying on the broken bed and the two pairs of big black, shiny shoes pointing towards the ceiling.

"I'll be back" he said to the bodies in his best impersonation of Arnold Shwarzenegger and ran out.

Chapter 7

Electronic City

Veenu's taxi was speeding along the elevated expressway on top of Hosur Road to Electronic City. Large office buildings appeared on either side of the elevated expressway. An ugly glass building with a hole in the middle belonging to an IT major appeared on the right indicating that they were almost there. Next to it was the famous pyramid shaped building also belonging to the same IT major. The taxi took the exit ramp which led them straight into Electronic City. To the left of the entrance was a board with a list of names of the Companies that had their offices here. It read like the who's who of the world's software companies. The entrance to the Info Systems campus was a little further ahead on the right hand side.

Veenu checked in with security. Having experienced the security at ITPL, he was prepared for the worst. He had the foresight to leave his laptop and bag behind. The security here was just as stringent at ITPL but since the security was for the entrance to the Info Systems campus rather than to an office park, they were better prepared for him. They knew he was coming for an interview and had his visitors badge ready. He needed to show them his photo id card and pass through a metal detector and he was through. He soon had the visitors badge around his neck and was being escorted across the manicured lawns to building 'A' where the interviews were to be held.

Suddenly Veenu screamed in pain and fell on his back onto the grass clutching the side of his head. He was sure that he had been shot by a long range rifle, the kind that has the cross hairs in its telescoping sight and the little red laser dot that appears on the target to visually show exactly where the bullet is headed. His eyes swam and his head spun. He fought the tears filling up in his eyes and managed to open them. His escort's face came into view. He was bending over Veenu, his face close to Veenu's. He was grinning. He seemed quite pleased with himself.

"Have I been shot?" asked Veenu.

"Shot? No. No. No." laughed his escort. "You have been hit by this golf balls."

He held up a white golf ball in front of Veenu's eyes.

"Did you know that we have our own private golf course on campus?" he said proudly. "Some of my colleagues are very good at golf. They can hit the balls very far."

Presumably Veenu had been beaned on the bonnet by one of these esteemed colleagues of whom his escort was so proud. Veenu felt the side of his head. It had swelled up into a painful lump.

"Do your good at golf colleagues always use unsuspecting visitors for target practice?" asked Veenu as he was helped up by his beaming escort.

"No. No" said his escort. He seemed hurt by this flippant remark. "They try not to hit anybody. They lose their balls if they hit a visitor."

"I agree that these guys should be punished severely for aiming their missiles at first time visitors to your campus" said Veenu. "But losing their balls?! Isn't that a bit too severe?"

Veenu's escort stared at him with a strange expression on his face but did not say anything. The rest of the walk to building 'A' was conducted in silence.

Veenu was asked to wait in the reception area. There were a couple more young software engineer types sitting there waiting for their turn to be interviewed. They were looking rather nervous and mouse like. Before Veenu could find himself a seat, a young, just out of college types walked out of one of the doors into the area. He was very clean shaven and fully dressed in an impeccable blue suit, red tie and shiny black shoes. The Japanese Gentleman probably wore similar clothes in his younger days.

The young man looked rather pleased with himself. He walked towards Veenu and waved a sheaf of bond paper at him.

"I got the offer letter" he said excitedly.

"Congratulations" said Veenu sincerely.

The other waiting, wannabe software engineers looked up enviously at the young man.

"What are *you* here for?" asked the young man noticing Veenu's stubble and then looking down at his 'used to be white' sneakers with disdain.

"I am here for an interview" said Veenu.

The young man smirked. "Good luck" he said sarcastically still staring at Veenu's shoes.

"I am off to buy myself a car" said the young man finally looking up again and sounding quite excited.

"Car?" repeated Veenu not quite connecting.

"Yes" beamed the young man waving the offer letter in Veenu's face again. "I just need this" he said. "With this offer letter, I can get instant financing at any dealer and have my car today itself."

"Congratulations" said Veenu again.

The other wannabe software engineers looked even more enviously at the young man, their mouths slightly open.

"Bye" said the young man. He smiled at everyone around and left the room smiling to himself.

Veenu took a seat and waited along with the others for his turn to be interviewed.

The young man was sitting across the table from a salesman at one of the numerous car showrooms on Hosur Road. He had chosen a fully loaded version of a mid size, red hatch back complete with a sun roof, as his first car. True to his word he had got approval for instant financing on the basis of his offer letter and was just about ready to drive out in his new purchase.

The monthly installments that the young man would have to pay for his new toy were somewhat higher than he had expected and the monthly paycheck he would be getting did not seem that high anymore. The car salesman had helped him calculate how much he would be getting in hand after all the taxes and Provident Fund deductions and it was not much higher than what he would have to pay to the car company each month. Still, the young man was pleased with his purchase. The car salesman had been rather nice and explained how if he lived frugally he could just about manage. And in any case, he could expect a big raise and maybe even a bonus in about six months time after which things would be quite comfortable.

"Oh kay" drawled the car salesman. "So you just need to pay me the registration, road tax and comprehensive insurance amount and you can drive off." He smiled encouragingly at the young man. "That comes to…" He pushed a piece of paper with some calculations in front of the young man. "That much" he said pointing to the total.

The young man looked aghast. "But… But I don't have that much money" he protested.

"Oh kay" drawled the car salesman. "No problem. I will tell you what. We can add this amount to your loan. That way you can pay it off slowly as part of your EMI (equal monthly installment)."

The young man nodded relieved. "Will that increase my EMI?" he said. 'EMI' was a new word he had learnt that day and he was quite pleased to be asking intelligent questions about it already.

"Yes" said the car salesman "just a little." He did some calculations and pushed a piece of paper in front of the young man. "Your new EMI will be that much" he said pointing to the figure on the paper.

The young man looked concerned again. "That is too much" he said.

"Oh kay" drawled the car salesman. "I see your problem. Let me see what I can do here." He leafed through a stack of papers on his desk.

"Tell me sir" he said finally. "Do you expect any monkeys to fall on your car in the next year?"

"Monkeys?" repeated the young man not sure if he had heard right.

"Yes" said the car salesman. "Do you expect any monkeys to fall on your car?"

"No" said the young man doubtfully.

"Perfect!" said the car salesman with a broad smile. "I think you should take this specially designed insurance policy. It is much cheaper than the comprehensive policy but has only minor exclusions. For example, it does not cover the damage caused by any living creatures such as monkeys, humans or other animals falling on your car. You are still covered for damage due to inanimate objects such as a rock or a dead monkey."

The young man still looked confused.

"The reason I am harping on monkeys" continued the car salesman "is because I had a case once where a monkey did fall on one of my client's car. You know that certain parts of Bangalore have a fair number of monkeys don't you?"

The young man did *not* know this but he said nothing.

The car salesman continued. "The monkey bounced off the car, landed on the road and got run over by a bus."

"That's terrible!" said the young man aghast.

"Yes" said the car salesman. "It was terrible. The car was badly damaged and the insurance company refused to pay!"

"We did argue that the exclusions were only for animate objects and since the monkey was now dead and inanimate, the insurance company should be coughing up the money but their point was that at the time the monkey hit the car, it was still a living creature and so they refused to pay."

The car salesman paused. "Any monkeys around your house?"

"No" said the young man doubtfully. He had arrived into Bangalore just a few days ago for his interviews and had not really scanned the surroundings of his current dwelling for the presence of monkeys.

"Good" said the car salesman sounding pleased. "Then I think we can take the risk. The policy also excludes damage due to drowning. Any chance that your car will drown in the next year?"

"Drown?" repeated the young man.

"Yes. Drown" said the car salesman. "As you know, basements in Bangalore can sometimes fill up with water when it rains."

The young man did not know this either but said nothing.

"I know of several cars that were parked in a nice dry basement. It even had a security guard stationed to guard the cars. He was sleeping next to the cars. But there was a thunderstorm during the night and by morning the basement was filled with water and there was no sign of the cars or the security guard."

"What happened to the cars?" asked the young man.

"Fully drowned" said the car salesman slowly. "Not even the roof was visible."

"And the security guard?" asked the young man concerned. "Was he also drowned?"

"No" said the car salesman. "He could sleep peacefully with all the water flowing into the basement so he left."

"Do you have a basement garage?"

"No" said the young man unhappily. "I don't even have a garage. I will have to park outside."

"That's *great*!" said the car salesman. "Then we are done. I will sign you up for this insurance policy and add the premium to your loan amount. Your EMI will hardly change at all!"

The young man still looked doubtful. Bangalore was starting to seem like a rather dangerous place.

"And after your raise next year, we can always switch you to the comprehensive policy" said the car salesman encouragingly. "So you just need to sign in a few places and you can be off in your brand new car covered by insurance!"

Sure enough, a few minutes later the young man had put on his seat belt and was off in his brand new red car. He made a mental note to himself, not to park in a basement, no matter how dry it was and he found himself involuntarily looking up at trees as he passed under them to make sure that they did not contain any unstable monkeys. But in spite of all that, he could not help but feel a heady power surge as he drove off in his new car. The broad grin of success was back on his face.

———◈———

Veenu was done with his interviews and was speeding along on the elevated expressway, on his way back to *the house with the green roof*. He was not sure how his interviews had gone. He thought he had answered all the technical questions well but in one case the interviewer had insisted that the complexity of any algorithm for the proposed problem could not be better than $O(N^2)$ but Veenu was sure that the algorithm he had come up with had a complexity of $O(N \log N)$. He had even provided a mathematical proof of this to the interviewer but the interviewer had not seemed convinced.

And the HR guy who had interviewed him over lunch seemed positively unhappy. He had asked Veenu why he wanted to join Info Systems and Veenu had quite truthfully replied that it was because he had been laid off from Corn Systems as the company had been shut down. Now, it turned out that the HR guy had actually heard of Corn Systems. He had read an article in the papers about their setting up in Bangalore and being at the cutting edge of failsafe security software. He had however not heard that Corn Systems had shut down and so was quite suspicious of Veenu's story. The HR guy had gone on to ask Veenu whether he was more interested in the kind of work that Corn Systems was doing or in the role that he was interviewing for at Info Systems.

Veenu had replied, "I was more interested in the work at Corn Systems but now that it has shut down, I thought I might as well try out the role that is available with you."

There was a period of silence after this answer. Of course that was most likely because the HR guy was hungry and was concentrating on eating. Veenu had tried to concentrate on his own eating during this time but the HR guy made him nervous. He kept looking at Veenu. Perhaps it was Veenu's style of eating. Veenu kept his spoon down after every bite, chewed for a while, then slowly picked up his spoon again, slowly filled it with the next installment of rice and then suddenly moved the spoon to his mouth. This style had evolved out of practical necessity since moving the food towards his mouth in a slow, lazy manner often caused him to spill the contents. But Veenu's style of eating was really besides the point. The point was that in his nervousness, he had managed to spill the HR guy's glass of water. It was a steel glass so there was no permanent damage but some of the water had fallen into the HR guy's food tray making his concoction of rice and sambar somewhat more watery than it already was. The rest of the water had fallen on the table and from there flowed onto the HR guy's lap. It soaked his pants in a rather embarrassing area. Water seeping around that area must have been rather uncomfortable but the HR guy had been quite nice about it actually. Veenu had come around to the other side of the table and helped soak up the water from the HR guy's lap with the help of some tissues. Veenu rubbed the middle part of his pants, hard with the tissues. "No problem, no problem" the HR guy said a few times in a squeaky voice while Veenu did this. Veenu wanted to soak up the water that had already seeped into the HR guy's pants back into the tissues but did not quite succeed, in spite of rubbing hard. The pants had a better absorption coefficient than the tissues.

The HR guy had not eaten much after this incident. He said he was full. So Veenu had sat and finished his food while the HR guy watched. Veenu was still quite nervous and did not want any more accidents so he had taken care to eat the rest of his meal carefully and slowly. In spite of the large amount of time it took for him to finish his food, the HR guy's pants had not dried fully and he got a few stares as they walked back to building 'A' together. The HR guy may have been a little uncomfortable but was quite good at ignoring the stares and looking straight ahead with a dour expression. On his part, Veenu kept a close eye towards where he thought the golf course was just in case any of the good golfing engineers were taking a break at the golf course after their lunch.

Veenu was sitting in his taxi, staring blankly in front of him as these thoughts went through his head. That's when he saw him. It was the Lava Crater Head Man! He was standing on the side of the elevated expressway, several meters in front of the taxi, and was happily clicking away as usual with his cell phone camera. He seemed to be taking particular interest in the ugly building, the one with the hole in it. An electric current flowed through Veenu's body at the sight of the Lava Crater Head Man. The swelling on his head where the golf ball had hit him began to throb painfully, not unlike Harry Potter's scar at the sight of Voldemort. The *signature suspense tune* had started.

"Stop!" Veenu shouted.

The taxi driver paid no attention.

"Stop. Stop" Veenu shouted more urgently. He sat up and shook the driver.

The taxi driver stopped. The car behind them screeched and skidded but managed to stop without hitting them. The car behind that swerved dangerously and honked loudly but managed to pass them safely on the right. Veenu got off the taxi and started to run towards the Lava Crater Head Man who was now behind them since the taxi had passed him before it had stopped. By now several cars had come to a stop behind the taxi and were all honking simultaneously. The Lava Crater Head Man turned around to see what all the commotion was about. He saw Veenu running towards him and started running away from Veenu.

Veenu gave chase. He was quite close to the Lava Crater Head Man now. The Lava Crater Head Man jumped over the boundary wall of the elevated expressway and landed on a ledge on the other side. Veenu jumped over the wall too. But he was a little behind the Lava Crater Head Man and there was no ledge in that part of the expressway!

The Lava Crater Head Man watched as Veenu fell into the thick traffic, on the road below the expressway shouting "Aaaaaaaaaaa" all the way down.

Chapter 8

The Police Again

Veenu landed feet first on the roof of a red hatchback. His feet hit the car just behind the sun roof. With a loud bang, the top of the car collapsed. Part of the sun roof flew off and hit the car in front. Veenu went straight through the collapsed roof and landed quite comfortably in the middle portion of the back seat of the car. The young man driving the car panicked and hit the brakes hard. The car behind them screeched and banged into the red car, smashing up the rear. In the meantime the impact of the sun roof on the car in front of them had caused that driver to stop as well. The red hatchback lurched forward from the impact of the car behind them which really had not done a good job of braking in time, and smashed into the car in front. The *signature suspense tune* stopped to allow everyone to listen to the full impact of the wildly honking cars and survey the damage. Luckily the young man who was driving the red car was wearing his seat belt and was not hurt at all but his car was in a shambles. Its roof had caved in. The sun roof had come off. The hatched back had been smashed inwards so that there was no longer any boot space. The front was smashed in as well. The hood had bent and opened up from the impact revealing more damage under it.

The young man who was driving the car was in shock. "What happened?" he said aloud to himself. "Something fell on the roof! Oh God! I hope it was not a monkey."

Veenu had just recognized the young man. This was the dude whom he had just met at Info Systems.

"Hi" said Veenu cheerily from the back seat.

The young man's nerves were already at edge. He jumped high at the sound of that "Hi" coming from the back seat and would definitely have hit the roof of his car, had there still been a roof to hit and if he were not wearing his seat belt. He held the steering wheel tight to try and steady himself and slowly turned his head around to look back.

Veenu beamed at the young man and said "hi" again.

"You?! What are you doing here?" The young man did not smile back.

"I fell from the expressway" said Veenu pointing upwards towards the almost non-existent roof. "Luckily I landed on your car. You saved my life!"

Veenu smiled again at the young man with genuine gratitude. But the young man was banging his head against the steering wheel. "Humans are living creatures" he said. "They are just as bad as monkeys".

Veenu felt quite worried about the young man.

The honking had died down. Several people had surrounded the red car. Several others were leaning against the railing of the expressway above and staring down. The Lava Crater Head Man too surveyed the mess below. He could see Veenu sitting comfortably in the topless car. Veenu seemed to be smiling? He shook his head in disbelief.

The Lava Crater Head Man must have been looking pretty intently at him because the lump on Veenu's head had started to throb painfully. He looked up through the broken roof to where the Lava Crater Head Man was just a moment ago, but he was no longer there.

———◈———

Veenu got off his cab in front of *the house with the green roof.* The multiple car accident had been followed by continuous incoherent shouting by the multiple parties involved. This had continued until the police arrived, after which each party and several onlookers had proceeded to simultaneously try and provide their version of the story to the police. To their credit, in spite of the several simultaneous explanations being offered the police did try to listen at first but soon gave up. The rant about how Bangalore was the only city in the world where cars routinely drowned and were pummeled by monkeys falling from the sky seemed to be the last straw.

Following standard procedure the police had impounded all the vehicles involved and asked the drivers to collect them from the police station where they would also be given a chance to officially record their statement. At the moment the police was not interested in listening to any of the stories. They were particularly not interested in the version which tried to pin the blame on monkeys and other creatures falling out of the sky. It was always better to wait until people had the chance to recover from their shock before officially recording any statements.

Veenu had shouted to the cab driver leaning over the expressway railing and managed to ask him to drive to the end of the expressway and wait there. He had then walked for a while until he found an auto which he took to the end of the expressway. The cab driver, since he had not been paid yet, was patiently waiting there.

And so here he was finally getting off the cab in front of *the house with the green roof* and paying the driver, inclusive of waiting charges which by the way were not inconsequential.

As Veenu's taxi had approached *the house with the green roof,* his thoughts had turned from the Lava Crater Head Man and the poor young man without the right kind of insurance for Bangalore city, to the bodies of the Japanese Gentleman and the would be assassin lying side by side on the broken bed, their bottoms resting comfortably in the V of the broken bed and their shiny black shoes pointing at the fan on the ceiling above. He felt thankful to the Japanese Gentleman for saving him from being choked by the assassin's rope.

He was now wondering if the Japanese Gentleman had come to and left for work or was he still lying there… next to the assassin? Either way he would still need to take care of the dead assassin's body. Probably the best course of action was to call the Chief Inspector and let the competent police deal with the situation and the body.

Veenu opened the door of his room. He stared at the broken bed. It was still quite broken but there were no bodies on it! Both the Japanese Gentleman and the assassin had disappeared! The broken lamp and the shattered pieces of glass were still lying beside the bed as proof of the morning's events but all the bodies had mysteriously disappeared.

Veenu scratched his head. He was thinking. The video of a possible sequence of events played inside his head. The Japanese Gentleman had come to. He was still groggy and his eyes were not focusing. His throat was paining and felt constricted, as if a rope was still tied around it and biting into it. He clutched his throat but there was nothing there. He managed to open his eyes fully and focus on the ceiling. There was nothing interesting there. He moved his eyes down from the ceiling until they were looking straight ahead and a pair of shiny black shoes came into focus. The Japanese Gentleman gave a bit of a start at the sight of those shiny, disjointed shoes framed against the bright light of the open window. He wiggled his toes and the shoes moved too. Yes, his own feet were in those shoes… and they were still responding to signals from his brain.

But what was that? Another pair of shiny black shoes was now visible to the Japanese Gentleman, somewhat closer and slightly to the right of the original pair. He wriggled his toes again vigorously. He moved his feet from side to side. Only the original pair of shoes moved. The second pair of shoes remained stationary. His feet were definitely not in those shoes. The Japanese Gentleman raised himself on his elbows to investigate.

He saw the ugly mug of the short assassin with the blackened bald head. The Japanese Gentleman jumped out of bed. The sight of this dangerous creature had caused a sudden spurt of adrenaline to flow through his veins causing his energy to return and his faculties to function at their fullest again. He stared at the assassin. But the dangerous creature was not moving at all. He extended a finger and gingerly touched the assassin on the nose. He quickly withdrew his hand again. But there had been no reaction from the assassin. The assassin had not moved. The Japanese Gentleman pressed the assassin's nose again with one finger. This time he kept it pressed for a while. There was still no reaction. The assassin seemed to be dead or at least nicely fainted. The Japanese Gentleman felt the assassin's wrist for a pulse. Yes, he seemed to be dead. Now what? The Japanese Gentleman looked at his watch. "Oho!" He was really late for work. His boss who was a punctuality freak would have his hide for this. The rope that Veenu had used to move the assassin's heavy body off of the Japanese Gentleman was still around the assassin's shoulders. The Japanese Gentleman caught hold of the rope and dragged the assassin off the bed. He put one end of the rope over his shoulder and walked out dragging the assassin's body behind him. The muscular Japanese Gentleman did not have too much trouble lifting the assassin's body and dumping it into the trunk of his Maruti Esteem. He was already very late for work and did not have the time to go to the police station right now. Perhaps he would stop by at the police station on his way back from work and hand over the body to them.

"Yes", thought Veenu as the video stopped playing in his head. "That is what must have happened." He realized that he did not have the phone number of the Japanese Gentleman and therefore could not call him to inquire about the body. He did not even know where he worked. In fact, he did not even know his name! He felt ashamed of himself. Here was a man who had saved his life and who he had been living with under the same green roof for the past two days and who had been trying to properly thank him for just as long. And all that Veenu had done was to push him away!

He ran to Vini's room. She would know what to do next. But her door was closed. The *signature suspense tune* had started.

Veenu knocked. He waited. There was no answer.

He knocked again. This time more loudly. Still no response. He tried the door knob. The door was locked. He stood staring at the door.

Vini was obviously not back from her interview yet. "Strange." thought Veenu "Vini has also disappeared". He took out his cell phone from his pocket and called Vini. Good. Her phone was ringing. But there was no answer. Veenu let the phone ring for a while until it timed out with a "… is not answering" message.

Veenu looked at his phone with disgust. "Now what?" he said aloud.

"Oh well" Veenu sighed. "I might as well do it." Veenu called the Chief Inspector.

"Halo" said a gruff voice. It was Mahalingam.

"Halo" said Veenu. "I mean hello. This is Veenu."

"Yes" said Mahalingam. "Mr. Veenu."

"I want to speak to the Chief Inspector" said Veenu.

"Why?" said Mahalingam.

"Why?" repeated Veenu. "Someone has died."

"Oho" said Mahalingam sounding pleased. "Another murder?"

"No. No" said Veenu quickly. "Not murder!"

"Then?" said Mahalingam. "Suicide?"

"No. No. No" said Veenu emphatically. "Not suicide."

"Then?" said Mahalingam gruffly not sounding pleased anymore. He was not interested in natural deaths.

"Someone got killed" said Veenu. "…by accident."

"Aha" said Mahalingam. "Someone got killed by accident" he repeated sounding sarcastic for the benefit of the Chief Inspector who was now listening intently.

"Killed by the Lava Man?" inquired Mahalingam.

"No" said Veenu. "I mean yes. He sent someone to kill me but he got killed instead in a fight. I did not mean to kill him. It was an accident."

"Oho. Oho!" said Mahalingam very pleased with this confession.

"Sirrr" he said excitedly to the Chief Inspector without bothering to cover the mouthpiece. "That Veenu fellow has confessed to the killing! Accidentally he says."

"Excellent. Excellent" said the Chief Inspector with a big smile. "Get him here immediately."

"Sir wants you here imm-ee-diately" said Mahalingam into the phone.

"But" started Veenu.

"No But" shouted Mahalingam. "Come here imm-ee-diately or we come and arrest you."

"Yes sir" said Veenu.

"Good" said Mahalingam. He hung up.

Veenu stared at his phone again. "Probably best to go to the police station and explain" he thought.

———◆———

Veenu arrived at the police station in an auto. The pot bellied policeman at the entrance was sitting on his chair leaning back onto the wall and just beginning a yawn as Veenu walked past him into the police station.

"Hey" an angry voice shouted from behind him.

Veenu turned around. The policeman from the entrance was right behind him looking quite alert.

"Mahalingam" said Veenu.

The policeman pointed inside with his thumb, yawned and walked back to his post at the entrance.

"That is obviously the password" said Veenu under his breath.

Veenu knocked on the Chief Inspector's door.

"Hey" an angry voice shouted from behind Veenu.

Veenu turned around. It was Ramalingam complete with his somewhat bigger belly compared to the cop at the entrance.

Veenu knew what to do. "Mahalingam" he said.

Ramalingam nodded. He knocked loudly on the Chief Inspector's door on Veenu's behalf and shouted loudly. "Mahalingam."

The door opened and Mahalingam's big belly emerged out of it. His uniform was as tight as last time.

Ramalingam pointed to Veenu.

Mahalingam nodded. He stood sideways in the door and said "come."

Veenu knew the drill. He squeezed sideways compressing Mahalingam's protruding belly in order to be able to enter and stood in front of the Chief Inspector's big wooden desk. The two tufts of protruding hair on either side of the Chief Inspector's head seemed to be protruding even more than the last time.

"Poor guy" thought Veenu. "He must have had a rough day."

Mahalingam ushered Veenu into a wooden chair in front of the desk. He then went and stood in his customary position beside the Chief Inspector, his belly resting comfortably on the table. The Chief Inspector picked up his pencil. The stage was set for the interrogation.

"So" said the Chief Inspector conversationally. "You are back?"

Veenu nodded.

"And you have confessed to killing the man at the restaurant?" continued the Chief Inspector.

"Confessed?. No.No." said Veenu shaking his head vigorously.

"Accidentally" said the Chief Inspector encouragingly.

"No" said Veenu. "I did not kill him. That was the Lava Crater Head Man."

The Chief Inspector scowled at Veenu. "Mahalingam" he shouted.

Mahalingam gave Veenu a stern look. "You confessed on the phone" he said.

"No. No" said Veenu. "That was a different man."

"What!?" said the Chief Inspector sitting up straight on his chair. "You have gone and murdered another man now?"

"Not murdered" clarified Veenu. I had to kill him in self defense.

"Self defense" scowled the Chief Inspector. "I thought you said it was an accident?"

"It was" said Veenu. "It was both."

The Chief Inspector's head fell on the table. He pulled at his hair. "Mahalingam" he said.

"Answer properly" growled Mahalingam.

"I think I should start at the beginning" said Veenu.

"Yes. Pleeease" said the Chief Inspector raising himself up hopefully.

"I was sleeping peacefully this morning" started Veenu. The Chief Inspector scowled. "Dreaming of Vini" continued Veenu.

"Aha" said the Chief Inspector. "Vini!" He snorted. "So your girlfriend is involved in this murder also?"

"She is not his girlfriend sir" said Mahalingam helpfully.

The Chief Inspector gave Mahalingam his choicest dirty look. Mahalingam shut up.

The Chief Inspector scowled at Veenu again. That was Veenu's signal to continue.

"I was sleeping peacefully this morning" began Veenu.

"SKIP THAT PART" growled the Chief Inspector.

"Yes sir" said Veenu. He paused wondering which part he should skip to.

"There was a knock on my door" said Veenu. "I thought it might be Vini but it was not." Veenu paused. The Chief Inspector was still scowling at him so he continued. "It turned out to be the Japanese Gentleman."

"Ok" said the Chief Inspector pleased that they were getting somewhere. "So is this Japanese Gentleman the one you killed accidentally in self defense?"

"No" said Veenu. "He is a nice guy."

"Then why was he knocking at your door while you were sleeping peacefully?" asked the Chief Inspector.

"Good point!" said Veenu.

"Why was he knocking at your door?" shouted the Chief Inspector.

"He wanted to say 'Thank You'" said Veenu.

The Chief Inspector's head was back on the table. He pulled at the two tufts of hair on either side of his head. Veenu and Mahalingam waited patiently.

The Chief Inspector looked up from the table. He looked dangerous. "You think the Bangalore police are full of idiots?" he said. "Come to the point. Whom did you kill?"

Veenu thought it best to come to the point. "It was the short man" he said.

"What short man?" growled the Chief Inspector, his head still on the table.

"I don't know sir" said Veenu.

"Mahalingam" shouted the Chief Inspector.

"Answer properly" Mahalingam growled. "Who was the short man?"

"I had never seen the short man before" said Veenu quickly "until he knocked on my door this morning."

"But you said that the Japanese Gentleman knocked on your door this morning" said the Chief Inspector.

"Yes sir" said Veenu.

"So the Japanese Gentleman is a short man" said the Chief Inspector hopefully.

"No sir" said Veenu respectfully. "He is quite tall actually. He also has hair on his head."

"WHO got killed?" said the Chief Inspector after he had finished pulling at his hair some more.

"The short guy sir" said Veenu quickly. "You see he knocked at my door. I thought it was the Japanese Gentleman come back to say thank you again. So when I opened the door I was looking for a tall guy but it was the short guy instead."

The Chief Inspector waited.

"I did not even see him at first but as soon as I looked down, he put a rope around my neck and tried to strangle me."

"Good for him" said the Chief Inspector strongly approving of the short guy's behavior. "So you killed him in self defense?"

"No. No." said Veenu. "Luckily the Japanese Gentleman arrived just in time to save me."

The Chief Inspector considered the facts. "The Japanese Gentleman accidentally killed the short guy while trying to save you?" he asked.

"No. No." said Veenu. "That was me."

The Chief Inspector was pulling at his hair again but Veenu ignored that and continued. "You see, after the Japanese Gentleman saved me, the short guy tried to kill him instead of me. I hit the short guy with the lamp but the bulb broke and got embedded in his bald head and his head started burning and became black. It was quite scary."

There was silence for a while. The Chief Inspector was thinking. Slowly he raised his head from the table.

"What about his body?" he asked.

"Oh. He had a great body" said Veenu. "Very muscular and broad shouldered. I am sure he had been working out for a while. His face was pretty ugly though with a big ugly nose. He looked quite scary with his burnt, bald head and ugly face."

The Chief Inspector's head was back on the table.

"But nothing wrong with the body" Veenu completed.

The Chief Inspector spoke with supreme control. He enunciated each word carefully and slowly. "*Where is the dead body?*" he said.

Veenu paused for a bit. "Disappeared" he said finally.

"What do you mean disappeared?"

"You see" said Veenu. "I was getting late for my job interview. So we lay the bodies of both the Japanese Gentleman and the short guy comfortably on the bed and left for our interviews. The bed was broken so they could not be completely comfortable but we did what we…"

"The Japanese Gentleman was also dead?" the Chief Inspector interrupted. His face was red.

"No. Luckily only unconscious."

"So" said the Chief Inspector raising his now purple face from the table and speaking in a soft menacing tone. "Am I to believe that you accidentally killed a stranger in self defense, arranged him neatly on your bed and went off to take a job interview?"

This did sound strange thought Veenu. "But Vini said that was the best thing to do" he said aloud.

"Vini!" snorted the Chief Inspector. "I thought you said that she was sleeping peacefully while all this was going on?"

"Actually she was" said Veenu. "But then I went and woke her up. No. Actually she was already up and dressed for her interview."

The Chief Inspector ignored this latest twist in the tale and snorted "Dead bodies don't just disappear into thin air on their own. Where did the body go?"

"I know where it went" said Veenu.

"You do?"

"The Japanese Gentleman came to and took the dead body with him to his office" said Veenu.

The Chief Inspector stared at Veenu. He was quite sure that Veenu was mad. He suspected it from his first encounter with Veenu but now there was no doubt in his mind. Still he persisted. "How did you know that the short guy was really dead?" he asked.

"I felt his pulse" said Veenu.

"Are you an expert at finding a pulse?" asked the Chief Inspector.

Veenu considered. He remembered that at first he could not find the Japanese Gentleman's pulse either and he had to check a few times before he could find it. In the case of the assassin he had checked only once!

"No" he said aloud doubtfully. "But he must have been dead. His bald head was completely charred and black and I am sure nobody could survive 220 volts of electric current flowing right into their brains?"

Then Veenu remembered that Vini had also checked and confirmed his prognosis. He brightened up. "Vini also checked" he said aloud. "She confirmed that he was dead."

"Vini!" exclaimed the Chief Inspector. "Is she an expert?"

"No" said Veenu softly.

"Where is this Vini anyway?" continued the Chief Inspector without listening.

"She seems to have disappeared too" said Veenu looking crestfallen. "She is not at home and she is not answering her phone."

The Chief Inspector nodded menacingly. He was sitting up quite straight now. "Enough!" he said. "I have had enough of your cock and bull story. Here I was thinking that I was the Chief Inspector of a peaceful locality. There had not been a murder in this area for the last two years and then you come along and in just two days the place is strewn with dead bodies."

"Strewn?" said Veenu hurt with the exaggeration.

"Yes. Strewn" repeated the Chief Inspector. "And we can't even find half of these bodies!"

"You know what I think really happened?" said the Chief Inspector after a pause.

Veenu did not say anything. He was feeling dejected. Unsaid fears had gripped his heart. Was it that the events of the last few days had finally caught up with him mentally or was it something else?

"I think" the Chief Inspector continued "that you are a paranoid and deranged mental patient who has been imagining that people are out to kill you."

Veenu shook his head shocked at the accusations but the Chief Inspector continued wagging a finger at him.

"That night you imagined that the man from the restaurant was going to kill you so you took out a knife and killed him instead as he was peacefully walking down the street."

Veenu looked aghast. The Chief Inspector was on a roll.

"Then to save yourself, you and that girlfriend of yours cooked up a preposterous story of a Lava Man and Orange Juice to put the blame on him"

"Tomato juice" corrected Mahalingam helpfully. He smiled at his boss. "And she is not his girlfriend."

The Chief Inspector thumped his fists on the table. His turned the finger that had been so far wagging at Veenu towards Mahalingam and wagged it at him instead. "Shut Up!" he shouted.

Mahalingam shut up.

The Chief Inspector had lost his train of thought. "Whom did Veenu kill?" he asked.

"The Software Engineer" said Mahalingam.

"No" said the Chief Inspector, "after that. Whom did he kill this morning?"

"The short ugly guy" said Mahalingam.

"Yes" said the Chief Inspector. "That short, stout, ugly killer with a rope" He hesitated slightly but resumed wagging his finger at Veenu and continued "was just a figment of our friend's paranoid imagination. Veenu's conscience forced him to call us and confess about the killing that night but then when he got here he lost his nerve and cooked up another cock and bull story to protect himself."

Veenu was looking very confused.

The Chief Inspector and Mahalingam both looked very pleased with themselves. The Chief Inspector was almost smiling.

"Arrest him!" the Chief Inspector directed Mahalingam.

Mahalingam whipped out a pair of handcuffs and clicked one of them around Veenu's right wrist with amazing alacrity. The other cuff he slipped around his own left wrist.

"Ha" exclaimed Mahalingam triumphantly.

Somehow Veenu did not have the energy to argue. He just sat there looking dejected. Both the Chief Inspector and Mahalingam beamed at him indulgently. The Chief Inspector finally had Veenu where he wanted him. As he sat there smiling at Veenu, the image of the computer screen with the photograph of the dead Software Engineer from the fingerprint match appeared in his brain. The Chief Inspector seemed to be thinking. Slowly the smile was replaced by his normal scowl.

"Ok" he said to Mahalingam. "Release him."

"What!?" said Veenu and Mahalingam together.

"Release him" ordered the Chief Inspector again.

Mahalingam reluctantly released Veenu. His expression was very similar to that of a fisherman that has just been asked to throw a big catch back into the water.

"Don't be too happy about being released" the Chief Inspector growled at Veenu. "If there is any other murder... or accidental killing or self defensive killing or any other form of killing anywhere in Koramangala, I will have you arrested and in jail before you can say 'Vini'. Understood?"

Veenu nodded.

"Take my cell phone number" said the Chief Inspector. "Call me *immediately* if there are any more incidents."

"Yes sir" said Veenu.

"Now get out of here" said the Chief Inspector. "We will be watching you."

"Yes sir" said Veenu. He slowly walked out of the police station. He was feeling drained and energy less. The lump on his head where the golf ball had hit him was throbbing with pain again.

Veenu reflected on his situation. Why was he feeling so low? For one thing, he had lost his job. Then he had lied to his parents. He could not bear to tell them that their brilliant son had lost his job on the first day! What would his father say? Of course he had managed to get an interview call right away but had dropped a whole glass of water on the HR head's head. No wait a minute. It had not really dropped on his head. Actually it was his thighs or actually ummm.... Actually it was the groin of the head of HR. Then he had gone and fallen on the brand new car of a brand new software engineer, wrecking several cars in the process. Besides that, assassins of all sorts, shapes and sizes had taken a fancy to him and were trying to kill him for no fault of his. Two people including one of those sweet software engineers were dead... because of him. And the police thought he was mad. Could he really blame them?

Now they were itching to arrest him at the slightest pretext. And there was no denying that he was now officially a killer! He had killed the would be assassin this morning, even if it was by accident. And how did the dead body disappear anyway? Was the assassin really dead? True, Veenu was not an expert in detecting a pulse. But Vini had confirmed? Vini! She was in HR. Did an HR course include training in emergency aid and pulse detection?

A new video was playing in Veenu's head now. It showed the assassin waking up from his unconscious state before the Japanese Gentleman did. He opened his eyes groggily and stared at his disembodied black shoes. Was that another pair of black shoes beyond his or was he seeing double? Yes, it was another pair. He turned his head. There was someone big lying beside him! He jumped and sat up straight. One of his latest would be victims was lying right beside him. There was a burning sensation on the top of his head. Now he remembered. There was unfinished business to be done here. The assassin assumed his favorite position on top of the Japanese Gentleman's chest, the white rope dangled behind him from his chest. He put his hands around the unconscious Japanese Gentleman's neck and started to press...

"No" said Veenu aloud shaking his head to get the horrible vision out of it. Could it really be that he had been foolish enough to leave an unconscious Japanese Gentleman neatly arranged next to an assassin and go for an interview! Was the Japanese Gentleman's dismembered body lying in a gutter somewhere? And he had not even been able to say 'Thank You' properly to Veenu. It was too horrible to contemplate.

Veenu had almost subconsciously hailed an auto while he was busy with his thoughts and was getting quite close to *the house with the green roof* now. He brightened a little at the thought of meeting Vini, running into her arms…. Well, maybe not quite that but in any case he would relate everything to her. She would know what to do next. He really hoped that she was back by now.

It was late in the evening and the sunlight was beginning to fade. Veenu entered *the house with the green roof* and walked toward his room. Somehow, instinctively he slowed down as he approached his room. The door of his room was slightly ajar. A sliver of light emanated from it. The *signature suspense tune* had begun.

Chapter 9

The Scream for the Dead

Veenu opened the door of his room just a little bit more. The door opened soundlessly. He peaked inside his room. His heart froze at the sight inside. It was Vini! She was sitting on the chair in front of his desk. She was staring at Veenu's laptop screen. The video of Vini's dance in the shower was playing on it!

Vini must have felt Veenu's presence in the room. She turned her head back to see who it was. Her eyes met Veenu's. A strange expression came on her face.

Veenu turned around and ran out. "Veenu!" he heard Vini shout. But he could not bear to face her now. He could not bear to face her ever again. She would never want to talk to him again anyway. What an idiot he had been. What was the need to pull off a juvenile stunt like videotaping her in the shower? He had not even gotten to see much of her because of all the blasted steam! Not only had he recorded her in the shower but then he had been foolish enough to not erase the recording and leave it lying around in his laptop where it could be easily discovered.

"And now she will never trust me again" he murmured to himself. "She thinks I am a pervert. A perverted, deranged, unemployed killer! That is what I have become."

Veenu had run out of *the house with the green roof* with his thoughts. He continued to run for a while without knowing where he was going. After a while he slowed down into a slow aimless walk. His cell phone rang but he did not seem to notice. Dark thoughts continued to go through his head. It had become equally dark outside, mirroring his mood.

There was a park on his left. The entrance was illuminated by a dim light. Veenu was feeling tired. He wandered inside the park and found a bench to sit on. The dim light from the entrance illuminated one side of his face. Long scary shadows moved across him as the occasional car drove on the road outside the park. It was the perfect setting for a depressed person to sit and brood.

Another disturbing thought squeezed itself in between the darkness into Veenu's head. "My laptop needed a password to unlock it. How did Vini manage to figure out the password?"

Veenu's phone rang again. He listened to the ring as if wondering where the sound was coming from. The phone rang again, this time louder and more insistently. Veenu fished it out of his jeans pocket. It was Vini calling. Veenu hesitated. The phone continued to ring. Veenu mustered up the courage to answer it. He braced himself.

"Sorry. I'm sorry" he said even before he said hello.

"Finally" said Vini's voice from the other end sounding relieved. "Where did you run off to in the dark? I have been calling and calling and you were not picking up your phone. I was soooo worried."

"Hai" said Veenu.

"What hai?" said Vini "why did you run away?"

"I…" said Veenu confused. "I thought you would yell at me."

There was a pause from the other end.

"For recording you dancing in the shower" said Veenu quickly.

"I **am** yelling at you" said Vini.

There was another pause.

"You IIT idiot (*IIT ka dhakkan* in the Hindi translation)" said Vini. "Did you think I have a habit of dancing every time I take a shower?"

"You mean…?" Veenu was wondering.

"Yes. I mean" said Vini.

"You knew?"

"Of course I knew"

Veenu was awestruck. "You are more intelligent than I thought" he said.

"Nice compliment" said Vini sarcastically. "You are stupider than I thought."

Veenu could not retort. "You dance well" he said.

Vini smiled. "Where are you?" she asked.

"I don't know" said Veenu. "I am in a park."

"Park? What are you doing in a park?" asked Vini.

"I am sitting on a bench" said Veenu.

"You are an idiot" said Vini. "Which park?"

"I don't know"

"What is around the park?"

"There is a light at the gate."

"And?"

"And there is a road next to it."

"You have been *extremely* helpful" said Vini. "Anyway, don't move. I will find you." She hung up.

Veenu stared at his phone. The display indicated that he had five missed calls. He checked the list. They were all from Vini. There were a couple of text messages too. Both were from Vini. "Where are you?" said the first. "Call me" said the second. Veenu had been so busy running away with his own dark thoughts that he had not noticed the phone ringing or heard the beep of messages coming in.

A Maruti Esteem car stopped outside the park. A figure jumped out of the passenger seat and rushed into the park. Veenu got up from the bench and took a step towards the oncoming person.

Vini threw her arms around Veenu embracing him in a tight hug. This time Veenu managed to put his arms around Vini as well. Several seconds later, Vini let go of Veenu, took a step back and looked straight into his eyes.

"Umm" said Veenu.

"IIT Idiot (*IIT ka dhakkan* in the Hindi translation)" declared Vini affectionately.

They both sat down on the bench that had been recently vacated by Veenu. They turned sideways facing each other. The romantically dim light lit up their faces. They stared into each other's eyes. There was something that Veenu really needed to ask Vini.

"How did you know that I was recording you?" he asked.

"Well" said Vini continuing to look into Veenu's eyes. "My suspicions were aroused when you kept saying – 'Take a shower in my room. Take a shower in my room'. Then when I came to your room that night, I noticed the wire going from near your laptop along the wall and disappearing into the wall near the ceiling. Then I knew for sure why you were so eager to have me take a shower in your room!"

Veenu nodded. He needed to ask Vini another important question.

"And, how did you find out my password?" he asked.

"That was easy" said Vini. "Remember, I got a laptop from Corn Systems too. It came with the same default password as yours. And you had not bothered to change it."

Veenu was impressed. This girl did have brains.

Vini and Veenu were still staring into each other's eyes. The *signature suspense tune* had begun. Their heads started to move closer to each other. Their lips were coming closer. Their eyes closed… But why did Vini get the strange feeling that they were not alone? Her brows wrinkled slightly in concentration. Their lips were slightly parted and almost touching now. Vini's eyes opened. Her eyeballs darted to the edge of her eyes and looked behind the bench. She screamed and jumped up!

Veenu's lips had just reached the spot where Vini's should have been. It was a comical pose. Sitting side ways on the bench, his head bent forward, his eyes closed, his slightly parted lips next to … nobody. He opened his eyes because of the scream. There was nobody in front of him. Was his breath really so bad that it had caused Vini to scream and jump up?

Veenu turned his head towards the front of the bench. Vini was looking aghast. She pointed behind him. Veenu turned around and looked behind the bench.

It was the Japanese Gentleman! He was standing there looking sheepish. He was not sure what to say. Seeing Veenu looking at him, he bowed and said "Thank You."

"You?!" said Veenu disgusted. "What are you doing here?"

"He drove me here" said Vini answering for the Japanese Gentleman.

"Drove you here? Oh. Ok." Said Veenu, "But why were you standing behind us and starting at us?"

"I did not want to distulb you" said the Japanese Gentleman.

Veenu did not look too happy but then he remembered the incidents of the morning and how the Japanese Gentleman had saved his life. He was quite relieved that the Japanese Gentleman was alive and that he had not been murdered by the assassin while he was still in an unconscious state lying next to the assassin in Veenu's broken bed.

Veenu realized that he really needed to thank the Japanese Gentleman for having saved his life. He stood up and following the proper etiquette for these things, he bowed and said "thank you."

The Japanese Gentleman bowed back. "Thank you" he said.

"No" said Veenu bowing again. "Thank *you*."

"Thank you" bowed the Japanese Gentleman.

"Thank you" Veenu bowed back.

"Thank you" bowed the Japanese Gentleman again.

"Stop it!" shouted Vini.

Veenu and the Japanese Gentleman stopped bowing to and fro.

"What are you two going on thanking each other for anyway?"

"He saved my life" said Veenu addressing Vini.

"He found my watch" said the Japanese Gentleman. "I have not been able to thank him plopelly." He sounded quite hurt about this.

"Ok" said Veenu who was feeling quite guilty about not allowing the Japanese Gentleman to thank him properly. "Please do thank me properly."

The Japanese Gentleman started to bow.

"Come in front. Come in front." Veenu motioned to the Japanese Gentleman to come in front of the bench. Veenu sat down on the bench and the Japanese Gentleman, still in his work suit and tie sat on his knees in front of him.

"Thank you" said the Japanese Gentleman. "You found my *pliceless* family watch."

"This" continued the Japanese Gentleman holding out his arm and pointing to his watch "was given to my gleat, gleat, gleat…" he was counting the number of 'gleats' on his fingers "gleat, gleat" he continued "glandfathel by the emperor of Japan. I am ashamed for *life* if it is lost. I am youl selvant for life for saving it."

The Japanese Gentleman addressed Vini now. He pointed to Veenu. "Him vely good man" he said almost choking as he said it.

"There. There" Veenu patted the Japanese Gentleman on his shoulder.

The Japanese Gentleman beamed.

Veenu beamed back. They spontaneously shook hands.

"Tell me your name" said Veenu after a somewhat elongated shake.

"Thang Wu" said the Japanese Gentleman.

"You are welcome" said Veenu. "What is your name?"

"Thang Wu" repeated the Japanese Gentleman.

Veenu looked bewildered. He scratched his head. "You have already thanked me more than enough" he said. "And I don't even know your name."

"Thang Wu" said the Japanese Gentleman again. "My name is Thang Wu."

"Oh!" said Veenu. He scratched his head some more. "Nice name!" he said.

The Japanese Gentleman beamed. "Thank you" he said bowing.

"My name is Veenu" said Veenu.

"Veenu" repeated the Japanese Gentleman in admiration.

Now that they were done with the introductions Veenu's mind went back to the incidents of that morning.

"What did you do with the body?" he asked.

"The body?" said Thang Wu San looking at himself but not really wanting to go into details of how he got himself a muscular body. Still if Veenu was asking, he had to answer.

"My fathel give me good body" said Thang Wu.

"No. No" said Veenu. "The *dead* body?"

Thang Wu did not understand. He looked at Veenu.

"This morning" explained Veenu. "After you saved my life from that assassin he tried to kill you. I hit him with the lamp and he got electrocuted. I left you and the assassin on the bed. You were unconscious and the assassin was dead. At least I think he was dead. Was he? Anyway where is he?"

Thang Wu shook his head. "I don't know" he said. "I got up. It was late. Velly late. I lan to wolk. My boss kills me if I am late."

"And there was no body next to you when you got up?" Veenu persisted.

"No" Thang Wu shook his head.

Dawn was just beginning to break. The camera panned onto the grand ITC Gardenia hotel in the heart of Bangalore city. This 7 star hotel is one of the few platinum certified green hotels in the world. This level of green certification requires 'living' walls covered with plants in most public areas. Most rooftops are covered with grass.

The hotel's palatial towers glowed with a gentle reddish hue in the breaking dawn. Almost all the residents of the hotel were still asleep and the lights in most rooms were off. But the lights were on in room 391. Inside it, the Lava Crater Head Man sat at his desk! His laptop was open in front of him. Photos of the bald, short man who had tried to kill Veenu were on the screen. His front, left and right profiles were clearly visible and marked as 'Front', 'Left' and 'Right' respectively. There was some text below the photographs that the Lava Crater Head Man was reading intently.

Four police jeeps approached the front gate of the hotel. Their sirens and lights were not on. Two of the jeeps positioned themselves strategically outside the gate while the other two entered the hotel gate. Hotel security was quickly waived with an impatient wave of police badges. The two jeeps positioned themselves at the lobby entrance. Mahalingam's maha belly was the first to emerge out of the first jeep followed by the rest of his body. Eleven other policemen emerged from the two jeeps. The policemen fanned out to man the different elevators and staircases in the hotel. The sleepy hotel receptionist looked up to see Mahalingam and two other policemen approach her at a rapid pace followed closely by the hotel security who were not really sure if they were allowed to let these guys through without the mandatory metal detector scan, even though they did appear to be policemen. The receptionist wondered how someone with a belly of that size could walk that fast.

In the meantime, the Lava Crater Head Man had got up from his desk and was staring at a big black suitcase that seemed to be carelessly strewn on the floor halfway between the desk and the bed. He knelt down beside the suitcase and unzipped it. He threw open the top. The body of the would be assassin was curled up inside it! The Lava Crater Head Man covered his nose with one hand. It had been almost 24 hours since the man inside the suitcase had been electrocuted and his body was beginning to decompose. Even though the expressions on the photos on the computer screen were not nearly as grotesque as the expression on the face of the body in the suitcase, it was clearly the same man.

There was a knock on the door.

The Lava Crater Head Man was taken aback. He was not expecting anybody to come knocking, especially at this hour. He quickly closed the top of the suitcase and zipped it up. There was another loud and impatient knock on the door along with a gruff "open up."

The Lava Crater Head Man moved to his desk and closed the lid of his laptop. He then moved to the door and peered through the magic eye. Three policemen with their guns drawn stood outside.

There was a loud thumping on the door. "Open up!" a gruff voice shouted.

The Lava Crater Head Man opened the door and stood facing the policemen.

A gun was placed on either side of the Lava Crater Head Man's head. Mahalingam slipped on a handcuff on his left hand, just as fast as he had done with Veenu. "You are under arrest" he said triumphantly. The other end of the handcuff was secured to his own hand.

The Lava Crater Head Man looked down at the handcuff. "Why am I being arrested?" he asked.

"For murder" said Mahalingam.

"But I have not committed any murder" said the Lava Crater Head Man.

"Ha!" said Mahalingam scornfully. "You can explain all that to the Chief Inspector at the police station."

There was a pause.

"Can I take my briefcase with me?" asked the Lava Crater Head Man pointing to a brown briefcase standing against the wall.

Mahalingam hesitated. "Ok" he said finally.

Mahalingam walked over to the briefcase with the Lava Crater Head Man and allowed him to pick it up.

"Ok" said the Lava Crater Head Man. "Let's go."

He was soon whisked off into one of the waiting jeep. A large contingent of the hotel staff and some early guests watched as the police jeeps rushed off, their sirens blaring and lights flashing.

The Chief Inspector was pacing up and down in his room, impatiently waiting for Mahalingam to arrive with his captive. Apparently the Chief Inspector pulled at his hair just as much when he was impatient as when he was frustrated so tufts of hair were standing up very straight on both sides of his head. They swayed in rhythm with his pacing.

There was a knock on the Chief Inspector's door. He pulled at his hair. "Come in" he shouted.

The door opened and Mahalingam's belly entered duly followed by the rest of Mahalingam and then his lava crater headed prisoner. The two escorting policemen also came in, their guns still drawn.

"Here he is" beamed Mahalingam.

"Excellent!" The Chief Inspector beamed back.

The Lava Crater Head Man was led to the chair in front of the desk that Veenu had occupied not so long ago. Mahalingam unshackled the handcuff from his own hand and shackled it to the chair instead. Then he assumed his usual position at the side of the Chief Inspector, his belly rested comfortably on the table. They were ready for the interrogation.

"So" said the Chief Inspector. He opened a drawer in his desk and pulled out the drawing that Veenu had made of the Lava Crater Head Man. He placed it in the middle of the table.

He looked at the drawing, then at the Lava Crater Head Man and back to the drawing. The tomato seeds on the Lava

Crater Head Man's forehead and nose were no longer there but still, there *was* a resemblance!

"Is this you?" the Chief Inspector directed his question to the Lava Crater Head Man pointing to the diagrammatic diagram that Veenu had drawn.

The Lava Crater Head Man stared at the drawing.

"If one stretches one's imagination" he said. "I suppose one could see a resemblance between this and anybody."

The Chief Inspector ignored this comment. "This used to be a peaceful neighborhood" he said. "But dead bodies at the rate of one a day have begun to appear" he paused "and some disappeared since you landed here sitting next to that Veenu fellow on the plane. Eye witnesses have seen you killing one of them in cold blood with a knife."

The Chief Inspector paused for effect. "What do you have to say for yourself?" he asked.

The Lava Crater Head Man was not sure. He pulled up his briefcase, which he was still clutching tightly with his non handcuffed hand and put it on the desk. All four policemen in the room stared at the briefcase.

"Let me explain" said the Lava Crater Head Man starting to open the briefcase. Then he stopped.

"Alone" he said pointing to Mahalingam.

The Chief Inspector nodded. "Out" he shouted at Mahalingam.

"But sir" started Mahalingam.

"Out" repeated the Chief Inspector gruffly.

Reluctantly, Mahalingam heaved his belly off the table and started to walk out.

"Out" said the Chief Inspector again, this time to the two gun toting escorts.

They all trooped out slowly.

In spite of the Chief Inspector's gruff manner and habit of trying to pull his hair out at the slightest pretext, Mahalingam respected him. Surely the Chief Inspector could not be bribed by a murderer, no matter how thick that briefcase was?

The Lava Crater Head Man waited patiently for the three policemen to leave the room and the door to click shut behind them. He opened his briefcase.

A few minutes later…

The Lava Crater Head Man was seen walking out of the police station, briefcase in hand, thankful for the reprieve he had managed to arrange but his brain was clouded with images of Veenu. "I will have to do something to get Veenu out of the way" he thought. He had a determined expression on his face.

It was rather strange. The Japanese Prime Minister was sitting on a horse. Nothing wrong with that I guess. Except that he was sitting on it bareback! That is, the horse was bareback, not the Japanese Prime Minister. And worse, he was sitting on it back to front facing the horse's rear. He was holding on to the horse's tail with both his hands. Veenu was standing directly behind the horse facing the Japanese Prime Minister who looked rather scared. Now where had Veenu seen that magnificent horse before he wondered? Ah Yes. It was on TV. The race horse that was about to win a race on

Bangalore's famous race track just before he had changed the channel. He would recognize that rear anywhere! What was the Japanese Prime Minister doing seated on this race horse? He was much too heavy to be a jockey.

"Help!" shouted the Japanese Prime Minister. He yanked at the tail and simultaneously clapped both feet down on each side of the horse as he shouted help. These actions made the race horse take off. The sudden acceleration caused the Japanese Prime Minister to lurch forwards towards the back of the horse. His nose crashed into the horse's back very close to its tail. He almost fell off but somehow managed to stay on.

Veenu gave chase.

"Heelp!" shouted the Japanese Prime Minister again repeating his action of yanking at the tail and banging his boots on the horse's sides, causing the horse to run even faster.

This was a race horse and a winning one at that so Veenu was not sure if he could keep up with it but somehow he managed to. The horse turned into the road leading to ITPL. The Japanese Prime Minister continued to shout "help, help" at regular intervals, while pulling the poor horse's tail and hitting it on the sides with his boots. The horse was gaining on Veenu. It turned into ITPL and whizzed past the open mouthed security guards at the gate.

"Stop" shouted the guards.

Veenu ran past the security guards too.

"Stop, Stop" they shouted and some of them gave chase.

It was a three way chase now. The horse with the Japanese Prime Minister on top was way in front with Veenu quite a ways behind and eleven security guards running behind

Veenu. The horse jumped over a neatly manicured hedge causing the Japanese Prime Minister to sway wildly, first forwards and then backwards.

The horse entered the Innovator building. BAWOOOM! There was a huge rumbling explosion in the building. The Japanese Prime Minister screamed. Veenu watched in horror as the entire building started to collapse on top of the Japanese Prime Minister.

"Noooo!" shouted Veenu aloud as he tossed on his bed in his sleep. Veenu was asleep on his broken bed in the customary face up position, his bums resting comfortably in the V of the broken bed. His own scream woke him up. His face was covered with sweat. His heart was beating fast. He sat up, with some difficulty since it was not so easy to sit on the slanting bed. He sat thinking for a while.

It was all clear to him now. What a fool he had been. He had read somewhere that men's brains stopped working when in the presence of a beautiful woman. Veenu's brain had been pre-occupied by Vini lately and he had not been thinking straight. The newspaper he had seen in Vini's room on the first day with the headline about the terrorist threat to Bangalore's IT infrastructure, the Lava Crater Head Man's presence at ITPL that day photographing the buildings there…. And the Japanese Prime Minister was scheduled to visit Bangalore. He had seen it on TV! It was all beginning to add up.

Veenu reached for the TV remote and switched it on. It was set to Fashion TV. A bikini model was sashaying down the ramp but this was not his immediate objective. He quickly changed the channels until he reached a news channel. It was running a show on the revealing scenes done by a popular new Bollywood actress. A particular clip was being shown again and again. "No." That was not the news he was looking for right now. He shook his head and changed to another news channel. "Yes." There it was. The Japanese Prime Minister had just landed at Bangalore airport! This local news channel was covering the event live!

The Japanese were impressed by Bangalore's meteoric rise as the world's software development center. The Japanese Prime Minister wanted to see the working style of a Bangalore software engineer in his natural work environment. The Japanese Prime Minister's first stop was going to be ITPL!

"Quick!" There was not a moment to lose. It would not do for the Japanese Prime Minister to be blown up while in Bangalore and take a good part of Bangalore's IT infrastructure and many of its famed software engineers with him. But what should he do? What *could* he do? Then he remembered that the Chief Inspector had given him his cell phone number during their last encounter. Veenu called the Chief Inspector.

Apparently the Chief Inspector had taken the trouble of entering Veenu's number into his for the Chief Inspector's phone displayed "Veenu" as it rang. "Yes. Mr. Veenu" said the Chief Inspector answering it.

Veenu was a little surprised that the Chief Inspector knew who was calling.

"Whom have you killed now" said the Chief Inspector.

"No, No. I have not killed anybody" said Veenu.

"But another dead body has appeared?"

"No" said Veenu. "No dead body. At least not yet."

"Not yet?"

"It's the Japanese Prime Minister. He is going to get blown up as soon as he enters ITPL" said Veenu quickly in one breath.

There was a long pause from the other side.

"Hello" said Veenu suspecting that he had been disconnected. "Hello."

"Yes" said the Chief Inspector. "I am still here. And how do you know all this? Are you involved in the plot?"

Veenu felt like he was implicating himself again but he persisted. "I saw it in a dream" he said.

"Saw it in a dream?!" snorted the Chief Inspector. "You think the Bangalore police consist of fools, do you?" said the Chief Inspector. "I don't know where you are getting your tips from but you are too late. We have known this for many days."

"What?" said Veenu flabbergasted. "You know that the Japanese Prime Minister is going to get blown up at the ITPL today?"

"Intelligence has warned us of a plausible threat to Bangalore's IT infrastructure. They have also warned us of a threat to the life of the Japanese Prime Minister while he is in Bangalore. The Japanese Prime Minister has made life difficult for us by insisting that he wants to see a fully functional software development center and not just an empty shell. But every precaution has been taken to ensure that you don't succeed in your plans."

"My plans?" Veenu blurted.

But the Chief Inspector was not paying attention. "Every inch has been scanned for bombs" he continued. "All equipment going in is verified to be bomb free. The place is covered by security cameras. It will be easier to bomb an air force base than ITPL" the Chief Inspector boasted.

Veenu remembered the immense security he had to go through to enter ITPL. Now it all made sense. The Bangalore police was not that foolish after all.

"Amazing" said Veenu reassured. "That's great. I commend you. The Bangalore police is not at all foolish!"

"Yes" said the Chief Inspector in a softer voice. He was taken aback by the unexpected praise and was not sure whether Veenu was being sarcastic but he was pleased nevertheless.

Veenu hung up. He was staring into space. The precautions seemed water tight. But something was still not right. Should he call the Chief Inspector again? No, he would never be able to convince the Chief Inspector. He would have to do this himself. But first he would have to get himself into that fortress called ITPL... and he needed to get there well before the Japanese Prime Minister did. The Japanese Prime Minister had already landed at Bangalore airport. Veenu looked at his watch. He needed to hurry!

He jumped out of bed. There was a whirr of color as he moved even faster than he had done when we was getting ready for his interview. When Veenu became visible to the naked eye again, his pink pyjamas and kurta top were lying in a heap on the floor and he was in his customary T shirt, jeans and used to be white sneakers.

Veenu rushed to Vini's room and knocked impatiently on her door.

"Come in" answered Vini sweetly from behind her door. "I have been expecting you."

"Expecting me?" Veenu was not expecting this response, and the *signature suspense tune* had begun.

Veenu turned the door knob slowly and flung open the door, stepping back slightly as he did so. Vini was sitting on the bed, looking lovely as usual. She was fully dressed and ready to go. She was casually dressed in a T shirt and jeans but still gave the impression of being dressed up. She smiled sweetly at Veenu.

"Why were you *expecting* me?" asked Veenu.

Vini was taken aback by the slight edge in his voice."It is a ritual with you" she said. "You rush in here every morning in your pink pyjamas."

"Oh" said Veenu.

"But today you are already dressed" observed Vini. "Any more dead bodies in your room?"

"Don't!" said Veenu. "You sound like the Chief Inspector."

Vini looked confused.

Veenu got to the point. "The Japanese Prime Minister is going to be blown up" he said "along with the Innovator."

Vini was really confused now. "Who is the innovator?" she asked.

"Not who, what" said Veenu.

This was not very illuminating for Vini.

"It's the building" explained Veenu "in ITPL." He looked at his watch again. "Look" he said. "There is no time for explanations." He grabbed Vini by the arm. "We have to get to ITPL."

"But…" protested Vini but allowed Veenu to lead her out of the room.

"Thank You must be leaving for work right now" said Veenu. "He works at ITPL."

Sure enough, Thang Wu San was just stepping out of the front door. He was dressed in his best suit. After all the Japanese Prime Minister was coming. Veenu ran after him. Vini followed.

"Thank you" Veenu yelled after Thang Wu. "Thang Wuuu."

Thang Wu was already at the front gate of *the house with the green roof* when he heard Veenu calling out to him. He stopped.

Veenu ran up to him. "You have to take us to ITPL" he declared breathlessly.

"ITPL?" repeated Thang Wu.

"Yes ITPL" confirmed Veenu. "We have to get there fast."

"ITPL impossible" said Thang Wu. "Not today. Only employees with valid photo id allowed inside today." He produced his photo id as he said this. "They will check at the gate. They check caal also. No bags allowed eithel. No laptops. Plime Ministel coming today." He beamed. "Velly stlict seculity! No visitols allowed."

Veenu nodded. He remembered how each car was being checked thoroughly that day when he had gone to ITPL.

"You have a Maruti Esteem" said Veenu looking at Thang Wu's car.

"Yes" said Thang Wu proudly. "I do."

"Come" said Veenu running towards the car. "Let's go."

"But?!" said Thang Wu and Vini both as they ran after him.

Veenu was at the car and trying the back door. Thang Wu pressed the button on his electronic key to open the car while still running towards the car. By the time Vini and Thang Wu reached the car, Veenu was already inside. He had climbed on top of the back seat and was looking out of the rear window.

Thang Wu peaked inside. "They check the back seat also" he said matter of factly.

"Yes" said Veenu. He got out.

"Now listen carefully. This is what we will do." He explained his plan. Both Thang Wu and Vini looked extremely doubtful. They exchanged skeptical glances but Thang Wu walked over and opened the boot. Vini looked inside apprehensively.

"How will two of us fit in there?" she asked.

Veenu surveyed the situation. "You will have to lie on top of me" he said climbing inside. He lay down on his back in the trunk. Vini climbed in and lay on top of him facing downwards.

Thang Wu closed the boot. He was still quite concerned. "I hope you will be fine inside" he said.

"Yes" yelled back Veenu. Vini did not say anything.

Soon they were speeding off towards ITPL. It was dark and cramped and sweaty and extremely uncomfortable inside the boot.

"I love this position" said Veenu.

"What?!" said Vini incredulously. Veenu was clearly at least half mad.

"I love your body on top of mine" said Veenu.

Vini gave him a dirty look that he could not see in the dark but settled herself more comfortably on top of him.

—◆◇◆—

Meanwhile, the Lava Crater Head Man was back in his hotel room. At that very moment he was sitting at his desk. His laptop was on his desk but the Lava Crater Head Man was facing the TV. It was tuned to the local news channel which was covering the Japanese Prime Minister's visit to Bangalore live! The Chief Minister of Karnataka was receiving the Japanese Prime Minister at the airport.

—◆◇◆—

ITPL was a long distance away. Thang Wu sped along as fast as he could. Each bounce of the car caused Veenu's back and bums to bump uncomfortably on the floor of the boot and Vini to get squished against him.

The road to IPL was lined with cops. With no visitors allowed into ITPL and some employees having decided to work from home today, the traffic was quite light. Soon all other traffic on this road would be stopped completely as the Japanese Prime Minister's cavalcade made its way on it. Still, it was a good half hour before Thang Wu's car stopped outside ITPL's entrance gate. Would they all be able to get past security? The *signature suspense tune* started. Vini and Veenu froze in the boot. They heard security ask for Thang Wu's ID. His badge number checked against a list of eligible employees. The guard stared at Thang Wu's face and made sure it resembled the one on his computer screen and the photo on the ID. He also made sure that the car license plate, make and color matched his records. He looked inside the car and made sure there was nobody else inside it. Finally he waved the car towards the car security check area.

Vini and Veenu felt the car start to move again. "Now!" whispered Veenu urgently. He pushed at the back seat from inside the boot. The seat folded over! A feature of a Maruti Esteem car is that the storage space can be increased by folding the back seat on top of itself. The boot and the back seat area can then be used as a big, connected storage space. Veenu had remembered that the security check for cars was a little inside the main entrance gate where IDs were checked. He had already unlocked the levers on the back seat of the car before leaving for ITPL allowing it to be folded by pushing from inside the boot.

Vini and Veenu quickly rolled over into the back seat and then onto the floor in front of it. The back seat was folded back into position and they both managed to scramble into a sitting position on it, trying to look as if they were tired of sitting there, as Thang Wu slowly pulled up behind the cars waiting for the security check. The sole occupant of the car currently being checked stood forlornly by its side as a swarm of security personnel did their job. They had opened all the doors of the car, its boot and even its hood and various kinds of detectors were being pressed into service.

"You go ahead" said Thang Wu loudly making sure the guard standing next to their car heard him. "I will join you aftel palking the cal."

Vini and Veenu got out of the car and walked towards the x ray screening area. There was a long line of people there. There was a separate line for people without bags. Even so it took Vini and Veenu another 7 minutes before they could get through the metal detector and thorough frisking. They walked off as fast as they could without arousing suspicion. Vini looked back at the security check point once they were a safe distance away. She heaved a sigh of relief. "Ok we are in" she said "now what?"

"Now, on to the Innovator" said Veenu. "Walk fast but don't run. There are security cameras everywhere. We don't want to attract attention."

They entered the Innovator. There were other employees walking in with them. They took the elevator along with some of them and got off on the 2nd floor. They headed towards the Corn Systems' office. There was nobody else going to that non functional office.

"Down!" said Veenu suddenly "on the floor."

Vini followed Veenu's lead and dropped down flat on the floor.

"Now we crawl" declared Veenu.

"What?" protested Vini.

Veenu raised himself slightly on his hands and knees and started crawling towards the Corn Systems' office. Vini followed his lead.

"And exactly why are we crawling?" she asked.

The image of the blinking red light on top of the Corn Systems' entrance door came into Veenu's head. He remembered the camera that had moved to focus on him as he had entered the office.

"There is a motion detector on top of the Corn Systems' entrance" said Veenu aloud "integrated with a camera that follows the movement. Most of these motion detectors are designed to detect humans while ignoring pets. That is both easier to design and necessary in order for them to not go off all the time when the owners are away from the house leaving their pets behind. So they ignore motion close to the floor."

"But why would ITPL security be worried about someone entering Corn Systems' office in particular?" asked Vini.

"I am not worried about ITPL security" said Veenu.

"Then why are we crawling?" Vini wanted to ask but did not. She was not enjoying this crawling around. It was uncomfortable and rather undignified. Nevertheless they continued to crawl.

Veenu got close to the wall and crawled along it as they approached the entrance. They were now next to the glass door covered with the brightly colored corn on the cob logo from top to bottom. Veenu looked up at the motion detector. It was not blinking and the camera pointed straight out towards the front of the door. Veenu pushed at the door gingerly and they both crawled in from the corner.

Veenu stood up once he was inside. Vini was glad to be able to finally stand up. The security guard was sleeping on his chair behind the front desk as usual.

"Shhh" said Veenu putting a finger on his lips. They easily tip toed past the guard into the room beyond.

They were in the enemy's lair! The *signature suspense tune* had begun. It was dark inside except for several multi colored LEDs flashing in one corner of the room. And all along the walls of the large room, close to the floor, green LEDs flashed intermittently.

Suddenly, the room was brightly lit! Veenu blinked in the sudden bright light. He looked around alarmed. Vini was smiling.

"I found the light switch!" she said.

"Oh" said Veenu. "Good job."

They surveyed the room. The large room was organized as an open office. One corner of the room seemed to be the IT center. It contained an internet router and an Ethernet switch. Several multi colored LEDs were blinking on that equipment. A continuous table top ran along the walls of the room. Flat computer monitors were arranged at regular intervals on the table top along with a keyboard and a mouse. A swivel computer chair was kept in front of each of the monitors. The CPU tower boxes were placed on the floor below the tabletop, still in their wheeled bases. Bright yellow Corn on the Cob logos covered most of each side of the black CPU boxes. A green LED flashed intermittently on each of the CPU boxes.

"Those are not computers" said Veenu pointing to the black boxes in their wheeled bases. "Those are bombs!"

Vini was not convinced about this dramatic proclamation from Veenu. She walked over to one of the keyboards and hit Enter. The black monitor, which had been in auto power off mode so far, came to life. A screen saver was running on it. A small corn on the cob appeared at the bottom left corner of the screen. It then made its way to the top right hand corner, getting bigger and bigger as it went. It exploded when it reached the top right corner! All the cob kernels flew away from the cob in random directions all across the screen. They ricocheted off the edges of the screen and disappeared in a mini explosion if they happened to hit each other. The sequence repeated itself when the screen was relatively free of corn kernels due to enough of them having destructed by exploding into other kernels.

"That's corny" said Veenu amused.

"Yes" agreed Vini "but it *is* a computer."

Veenu stared at the blinking lights on the internet router in one corner of the room.

"These are integrated bombs cum computers" he declared. "They are being controlled over the internet. As soon as the Japanese Prime Minister walks into the building, a signal will be sent to the computers over the internet and they will all explode!"

Vini stared at Veenu.

"Don't you see?" continued Veenu. "This room is right in the center of the building directly over the ground floor where the Japanese Prime Minister will walk into. The bombs are carefully arranged on the floor and next to the pillars. When they explode, the whole floor will be blown away on top of the Japanese Prime Minister. But that will only be a small part of the tragedy. The pillars will collapse and the weight of the building from the top floors will cause the entire building to collapse into its hollow center. All the employees in the building will die. An icon of Bangalore's IT infrastructure will disappear and several people around the world who depend on 24/7 phone support from the people working in here will be left on hold on their phones."

Vini was aghast. "It's horrible" she said.

"It's brilliant" agreed Veenu.

"Ookay" said Vini thinking aloud. "So all we have to do to save the world is to switch off these damn computers."

She leaned forward towards one of the power switches on the wall.

"Nooooo" shouted Veenu. He moved like lightning and grabbed Vini's hand just as it was about to reach the switch. "Don't" he said loudly.

"Ouch" said Vini "that hurrrt! What's the big deal?" She looked angrily at Veenu.

Veenu had remembered that Dr. Suresh Sharma of Corn Systems was an expert in power off fail safe security systems from what he had researched on the internet.

"If you switch it off, the bombs will explode" he said aloud. "Suresh Sharma, one of the founders of Corn Systems was an expert in designing power off, fail safe systems. I am sure these computers are designed to work on capacitor based residue power for a short amount of time after a power failure. That short amount of time is commonly used to save your unsaved documents so that you don't end up losing your work just because there is a power failure in the middle of your typing. But (he paused for breath) the same technology can be used to cause an integrated bomb to explode... and I can bet that it has."

"In other words" said Vini. "No switching off these things."

"Right" said Veenu.

Vini considered their situation. At any moment now the Japanese Prime Minister would walk into this building and...

"But how?" she voiced her latest thought aloud. "How will these all knowing computers know when to explode? I mean how will they know that the Japanese Prime Minister has entered the building? Don't tell me that there is some exotic face recognition technology linked to the security cameras at ITPL that somehow feeds into these computers?"

Veenu shook his head slowly. "No" he said. "It is much simpler than that. Remember that the local news channel is covering the Japanese Prime Minister's visit live? You can be sure that at this very moment there is someone out there sitting comfortably on a sofa watching TV! He will know when the Japanese Prime Minister has entered the building and then all he has to do is to move over to his laptop and click on the 'detonate' button. The command will be sent to all the computers in here over the internet and boom!"

"At this very moment" – Veenu's words sent a chill down Vini's spine. How many moments more did they have before they were both blown up?

"That's horrible" she said aloud. "The internet is a terrible thing!"

"It is just a tool" said Veenu. "You can use it for good and you can use it for evil."

Vini nodded. Another idea was forming in her head. "If these things will be told to explode over the internet" she said to Veenu pointing to the RS232 cables coming out of the computer boxes, "why don't we just unplug that internet cable? The computer will no longer be connected to the internet and so it will be unable to receive any blow up command over the internet and…"

She stopped. Veenu was shaking his head. "Nope" he said.

"Why not?" said Vini exasperated.

Veenu pointed to the green LED on the nearest computer. It had just blinked. "See" he said. "That green light just blinked."

"Yes" said Vini. "It means that the computer is on."

"That is the Ethernet LED" said Veenu. "It blinks when there is data being transmitted over the Ethernet."

Vini looked at Veenu quizzically. "So?" she said.

"So" said Veenu. "If these computers are just sitting here waiting for the detonate command, there should be no reason for them to be communicating over the internet.

"And" he continued after a slight pause "that LED blinks every 5 seconds."

Vini was starting to understand… Or maybe not. She looked confused.

"That means" said Veenu, "that there is a program running on each of these machines that is communicating over the internet every 5 seconds. I can bet that it is the program that is controlling the bomb. It is sending an ack or an 'I'm alive' message to its master every 5 seconds."

Vini was beginning to get it now.

"If the RS232 cable is disconnected or if the computer is switched off, the master will stop receiving the ack. I am sure that if that happens, the master will automatically send the detonate command to all the other computers in this room. They will explode and"

"And no more Innovator" completed Vini. "Yes I know."

Vini looked grave but she had not given up quite yet. She was thinking. She had another idea!

"What if we just switch off that router thingy?" she said brightly. "That way *none* of the computers will have access to the internet. So 'the master' will not be able to send the detonate command to *any* of them.

Veenu shook his head. (He was really irritating Vini now.) "Normally acks expect to get back an ack-response" he said. "If this is a well designed fail safe system, which I am sure it is, then the bombs will explode autonomously if they don't receive the ack-response."

Vini scowled. "So" she said. "What you are saying is that there is *no way* to keep these things from exploding?"

Veenu nodded. "You got it" he said.

Vini was getting really angry now. "So you made us squeeze into the boot of that stupid smelly car and bounce all the way here, then crawl like animals into this place just so that we could get blown up?"

Veenu did not say anything.

"Whose side are you on anyway?" completed Vini.

Veenu did not say anything. He looked quite sad.

The enormity of the situation was beginning to seep into Vini. She had so far assumed that Veenu had a plan and they would diffuse the bombs, save the world and be out of there in a jiffy. Now it seemed that there really was no way to diffuse these bombs. Did they really have just a few moments to live?

"How long do we?" Vini choked slightly and could not complete her question. She moved closer to Veenu and put her arms around him in a tight embrace. Her cheeks touched his. "How long do we have to live?" she asked softly.

"Let's find out" said Veenu decisively. He disentangled himself from Vini and sat down on the swivel chair in front of the nearest computer screen. A corn loaded with corn kernels had just exploded in the top right corner of it and corn kernels were flying around all over the screen. Three pairs collided almost simultaneously resulting in three simultaneous mini explosions in three different parts of the screen. Veenu hit Ctrl-Alt-Del. The screen saver gave way to an unlock prompt. The user name was already filled in but Veenu needed to type in the password. Veenu stared at the screen for a second. He typed in something and hit Enter. The password was correct! The screen unlocked.

Vini, who was leaning over Veenu's shoulder was impressed. "How did you know the password?" she asked.

"You taught me that trick" said Veenu. "It's the same as the default password our laptops shipped with!"

Veenu started up a browser and typed in a URL. The page that loaded was divided into different sections with titles such as "Sports", "Entertainment", "News", "Music" etc. Under each title was a list of TV channels for that type of programming with the logo of the TV channel next to it. Veenu clicked on the "Channel 9" link in the news section. A video started up in the browser and brought up Channel 9 – the local news channel!

"You can get live TV on the internet?" exclaimed Vini.

"Not all channels" said Veenu. "But yes, you can stream in several channels from around the world for free. It is not very well advertised. You need to know where to look."

Veenu clicked on the full screen icon on the video player and they watched TV for a while. The Japanese Prime Minister was on his way to ITPL from the airport. He seemed to be about half way there.

"From where he is it would have taken him about an hour to get here in normal Bangalore traffic but they are clearing the roads for him so he should be here in about… 20 minutes" said Veenu.

Veenu got out of full screen mode and clicked some things and did some resizing to get rid of the browser cruft around the video player and moved the window so that they could follow the Japanese Prime Minister's progress towards doom in the top right hand corner of the screen.

"Twenty minutes to live" said Vini. "Now what?"

Veenu was thinking. "First we need to find out which program is controlling the bomb" he said.

He started up the "Task Manager" and quickly scanned all the running processes. Vini looked too. All the usual suspects such as "explorer.exe", the browser and several system processes you would normally expect to see on a PC showed up in the list.

"Nothing suspicious" said Vini. "How do we know which process?"

Veenu brought up a Command Window. He typed

netstat –b –o

A list of open internet sockets showed up along with the executable name and process id associated with them. There were not too many of them. The browser was in the list of course and so was the video player and then there was a 'rundll.exe" that was connected to IP address 77.5.18.13.

"Voila" said Veenu pointing to 'rundll.exe' in the list. They have cleverly called the bomb program 'rundll". You can normally expect a few instances of that in the process list of a normally running PC. But it does not usually connect to an external IP address. This is definitely the bomb controller masquerading as a normal system process."

Vini was impressed. "So now can we prevent the bombs from exploding?" she asked hopefully.

"Maybe" said Veenu, "if we kill the process then it can no longer detonate the bomb."

"But" said Vini, it was her turn to point out the obvious flaw in this plan. "If we kill the process, won't it stop sending those ack thingies to the Master?"

'Yes" said Veenu.

"And that will cause all the other bombs to explode?"

"Yes" said Veenu.

"So?" Vini was perplexed again.

"So we need to kill this process on ALL the computers simultaneously" said Veenu. "Or at least kill them all within five seconds of each other."

Vini looked around. There was no way the two of them could kill this process on all 20 computers in the room within 5 seconds even if they set things up first such that they just needed to hit 'Enter' in a command window in each of the computers to kill the process. Even then they would need to physically go to each of the computers and hit 'Enter'. There was no way they could do that within 5 seconds.

"But that's impossible" she said aloud. "How are we going to kill all the processes within 5 seconds of each other?"

"Impossible" repeated Veenu. "Yes, but not if we do it programmatically."

"How?"

"I will have to write two programs" said Veenu. "The first will be the killer app. We will need to physically install it and run it on each machine. It will figure out the bomb controller process using logic similar to what we just did using *netstat*. It will then wait for a signal from the 2nd program – The Killer Master. When all the killer apps are ready and waiting, I will launch the Killer Master which will broadcast a signal to all the computers over the Ethernet. The killer apps will receive the signal and simultaneously kill the bomb controllers."

"Sounds complicated" said Vini doubtfully. "Will it work?"

"Will it work?" That was a good question. Veenu was extremely doubtful that it would work but for different reasons than Vini. Veenu was sure that given sufficient time he could write the program he had just described and that it would work. The problem was *time* or actually lack of time. He had maybe 15 minutes to write both programs. There was no time to debug them so they would both have to work perfectly the first time. Veenu tried to remember when was the last time he had written any piece of code, even a small piece of code that had worked perfectly the first time he had tested it. He could not think of any! The clear answer was 'never'. And that was not all. There was no remote procedure call or other remote control facility available on these computers so once written the killer app would have to be physically copied onto each of these machines. That would take time too. There were two of them. They would have to cut down the time required by some kind of parallel processing. But how? Vini could not write the programs and she could not start copying them until the killer app was ready.

He turned to Vini. "It *has* to work" he said sounding much more confident than he felt. "But I need your help. We need to make sure we don't waste any time copying these killer apps to each of the 20 computers. So here is what you need to do. While I am coding the app, unlock each of the computers and disable the screen saver." Veenu was sharing the C drive as he said this. "Then map a drive letter on each of the computers to the C drive on this one. Call it Z:.

"How do I do that?" Vini interrupted.

Veenu showed her.

"Then" continued Veenu, "start a cmd window and type the following on it."

Copy z:killer.exe .; killer.exe

"Then all you have to do when the killer app is ready is to hit Enter in each of the command windows. You can do that while I am writing the Killer Master."

Viini nodded. She got to work, starting with the computer next to Veenu's. She would have to work fast.

Veenu looked at the TV feed on the upper right corner of his screen. The Japanese Prime Minister's journey to ITPL was not considered interesting to cover and the programming had switched to Japan and the state of the Indo-Japanese relationship. Veenu reckoned that he had maybe 14 minutes before the Japanese Prime Minister arrived. This computer seemed to have the same basic install image as his laptop. He brought up the C++ programming environment that he knew would be on the computer since it had the same install image as his laptop.

He had always wanted to write a killer app and he would finally be doing just that. He would have to program at high speed and without making any mistakes. There would be no time to test or debug his program and the stakes were high. All the people in the building would pay for even one mistake with their lives. He needed to be calm and concentrate. He closed his eyes and took a few deep breaths.

He opened his eyes. It was him and the computer now. Nothing else mattered. He started writing code at high speed. First get the list of open internet connections on the computer. Then check the IP address of the connection. Find the one that was connected to 77.5.18.13. Get the process id for that process. Print a message saying "bomb process found". Then open a socket on a random port number, say 1179 and wait to receive a message. Once a message was received, kill the bomb process and print a message saying "Bomb Disabled!".

Ten minutes had gone by. He glanced at the upper right hand corner. The live feed was on again. "Oh God!!" He had over estimated the time he had. The Japanese Prime Minister was already entering ITPL! He looked around. Vini still had about 5 computers to set up for the copy. Sweat broke out on his brow. He hit the compile button. "No!" There were syntax errors in his code. The Japanese Prime Minister had entered ITPL and was moving towards the Innovator accompanied by his entourage that included the Chief Minister of Karnataka! Veenu quickly corrected the error and hit compile again. "Nooo" There was still one more error. "Calm down" he told himself. He fixed the remaining error and hit build. This time, the program compiled and linked without errors.

But the Japanese Prime Minister was already at the entrance of the Innovator. Alas, they had run out of time. They would soon be dead! He turned around and looked at Vini. She was still diligently setting up the last few computers, blissfully unaware that the Japanese Prime Minister was already here. Veenu waited for the inevitable. Vini looked beautiful.

———◆———

Even though he had turned down the volume on the video player while he was concentrating on coding, he heard the commentator say "The esteemed Prime Minister of Japan, Shinko Motu San is about to enter the iconic Innovator building at the International Tech Park in Bangalore." He turned around. The Japanese Prime Minister had stopped just outside the Innovator for a photo op! The Japanese

Prime Minister and the Chief Minister of Karnataka both had wide grins on their faces for the TV cameras.

Quick! Perhaps all was not yet lost. He quickly copied the exe he had just created to C:\ and typed 'killer' in the command window. He held his breath and hit 'Enter'. The words "bomb process found" appeared in the command window! Presumably the killer app was now waiting on port 1179 for a message. At least the first part of the program seemed to have worked.

He looked around. Vini still had 2 computers left to set up. He still needed to write the Killer Master. How long would that take? But wait, maybe there was an easier way. He hit CTRL C in the command window to kill the running killer app. Instead of waiting on a socket, the killer app could simply look for the presence of a file on Z:. He quickly modified the code to busy loop and look for a file called Z:\Kill or C:\Kill. The killer app would go and kill the bomb process as soon as it found the Z:\Kill or C:\Kill file. That way he did not need a 2nd program. All he needed to do was to create a file called C:\Kill on this computer which would map to Z:\Kill on the others.

He compiled and ran the program again. "bomb process found" it said again.

Vini was setting up her final computers now. "Start copying" Veenu shouted to her. "The Japanese Prime Minister is already here."

Vini ran over to Veenu.

"They have stopped for the cameras just outside the Innovator" said Veenu pointing to the TV screen. There was urgency in his voice. "We may not have much time."

Vini ran back to the computers she still needed to set up. She set up the connection to Veenu's computer and copied over killer.exe. She ran the program. The words "bomb process found" appeared in the command window. Vini smiled. She moved onto the next computer and hit enter.

Veenu stared at the T V screen. The Japanese Prime Minister had started to move into the Innovator.

"He is moving in!" Veenu shouted with urgency. "I will take half of these" He ran to the computer next to him and hit Enter and without waiting for it to print anything he ran to the next one and hit Enter. His brow was covered with sweat. Vini and Veenu met at the other end of the room.

"Quick" said Veenu. I need to create a file called 'Kill'. Both of them ran over to the other side of the room to the computer that Veenu had been working on. The Japanese Prime Minister was already in the center of the main hall of the Innovator. The terrorist in charge of this operation must be ready to hit the 'Detonate' button just about *now*. Will they be able to kill the bomb programs before that command made its way over the internet to these computers? With trembling fingers Veenu created another Command Window and typed '*echo* > *C:\Kill*'. He hit Enter. Would it work?

Vini and Veenu stared at the computer screen for what seemed like an eternity. The Japanese Prime Minister was past the center of the building now. The words "bomb disabled" appeared in the Command Window! Vini and Veenu looked at the computer next to them. "Bomb disabled" it said. All the computer screens around them had the same words on them now "Bomb disabled."

"You did it!" Vini shouted, a big smile on her face. She raised her hand for a high five. Somehow Veenu still could not believe that they had actually pulled this off. "Bomb disabled" was just a message that his program printed. But had it really worked? He looked at the TV screen. The Japanese Prime Minister had definitely walked past the center of the building now. He grinned and met Vini's hand in a loud high 5.

But the sound of the clap of their hands was drowned by the noise from a HUGE EXPLOSION!

The lights went out. The wall behind Vini had broken up and pieces of it were flying towards her at high speed but clearly visible to the viewer as the playback was in slow motion mode now. Veenu grabbed Vini and pulled her down to the floor. He maneuvered himself as they were both coming down so that he landed on top of her and covered her body with his. Most of the debris from the shattered wall flew harmlessly over them.

The deafening sounds from the explosion and the flying debris had given way to a deathly silence. There was no air conditioning running any more and no sound from the computers either. It was pitch dark.

"It felt like a… like a tomb!" Vini could not keep the thought from completing. Veenu felt heavy on her.

"Get off me" she said aloud pushing at him.

There was no answer.

"Veenu?" she said again.

Hesitatingly her hand went up his limp body searching for his neck. Veenu was covered with debris. A long piece of broken wood lay on his neck and head.

"Veeeenuu!!" Vini's scream reverberated in the darkness. It was a scream for the dead.

Chapter 10

The Lava Crater Head Man

Three days later…

The Lava Crater Head Man was sitting in room 391 of the ITC Gardenia hotel. He was watching TV! It was tuned to a news channel.

"It is now clear" the news reader said "that the explosion at the ITPL was caused by a terrorist bomb as part of an elaborate and sinister plot, not only to kill the Japanese Prime Minister and the Chief Minister of Karnataka but also to bring down and obliterate the entire Innovator building at the ITPL." The visuals on the TV screen showed the International Tech Park and the majestic buildings inside it. "Along with thousands of software engineers inside it. Had the terrorists succeeded in their dastardly plan, it would have caused irreparable harm to India's economy by delivering a body blow to the booming software sector. There were a total of twenty one bombs set to go off simultaneously on that fateful day, designed to explode as soon as the Japanese Prime Minister and the honorable Chief Minister of Karnataka entered the Innovator building. However the terrorists had not counted on one fine young man." A passport picture of a smiling Veenu covered the TV screen.

"Because of this man, twenty one bombs did *not* explode on that fateful day. Instead only one bomb exploded! The other twenty bombs were disabled just in the nick of time by this brave young man. This young man, who is now being hailed as India's greatest hero of the twenty first century. Even as that one bomb exploded, his only thought was to save the lives of those around him. Veenu managed to save the life of his companion Vini by protecting her with his own body."

"But alas that one bomb did manage to kill one man and could still claim another victim. Veenu himself continues to be in a coma battling bravely for his life! The whole nation is praying for Veenu's recovery. From Kashmir to Kanyakumari special prayers and yagnas are being organized to compel the gods to save Veenu's life."

The words "Breaking News" flashed red and bold on the TV screen.

"We now take you live" said a newscaster "to Manilal hospital where a crowd is keeping a 24 hour vigil outside the hospital. Our correspondent, Deepti Chaya is present live at the scene."

"Deepti, what is the mood of the people there?" What are they saying?"

The scene shifted to Manilal hospital. There was indeed a crowd gathered outside it. There were several people standing behind Preeti Chaya waiting to air their opinion live on national television. In the corner of the screen one could see another set of people purchasing roasted peanuts (*moong fali*) from a vendor.

"The mood here is extremely somber but determined" said Deepti. "People are categorically saying that they will not leave until Veenu comes out of the coma."

"But I will let our viewers hear it with their own ears." She turned to the man standing to her right. "Why are you here?" she asked "and until when will you stay here?"

The man spoke loudly and passionately into the mike. "We are demanding that the doctors work day and night to bring Mr. Veenu out of the coma. There must not be any let up in the treatment given to him." He raised his voice further. "We will *not* go until Veenu comes out of his coma."

"Veeenu" he shouted into the mike.

"Zindabad" shouted the crowd behind him.

"Veeenu."

"Zindabad."

Deepti took the mike back. "As you can see" she said the people are really concerned and rooting for their hero, Veenu."

She turned to the man on the left who had been waiting patiently so far. "What are you planning to do to help the country's hero?"

"We are all going on a hunger strike" declared the man pointing to a group of people behind him who all nodded in agreement. "Veenu is lying there on a hospital bed in a coma" said the man, his voice choking with emotion. "He is not able to eat or drink anything. We will also not eat until he eats."

"Do you think that will help Veenu?" asked Deepti.

"Yes definitely" said the man forcefully. "God loves sacrifices. Our fast will go a long way in helping our Veenu come back to life."

"So, there you have it" said Deepti taking the mike back and facing the camera. "People out here are fasting and praying and generally doing everything possible to make sure that Veenu comes out of his coma quickly. Back to you Charkha."

The Lava Crater Head Man picked up his gun from the table next to him. He pointed it at the TV screen and pretended to shoot it. "Bang" he said as he switched off the TV using the remote in his other hand.

He sat deep in thought caressing his gun.

⚬

At this point Veenu was in one of the VIP category rooms in the hospital. He was lying motionless on the hospital bed in the middle of the room. His nose and mouth were covered by an oxygen mask. His head was covered with bandages. A drip was attached to his hand. The monitor next to him showed a steady heartbeat and beeped at regular intervals.

Vini and Veenu's sister were sitting on plastic chairs next to his bed. His mother was sitting on the attendant's bed next to the wall. Her head was in her hands. Veenu's father was pacing up and down the room, rather disconcertingly.

Two constables were on guard outside the room. They had been posted there to prevent any visitors, journalists or terrorists from entering the room without permission. A man in a white overcoat was walking towards the room. The *signature suspense tune* had started.

The man in the white overcoat slowly approached the closed door of Veenu's room. One of the constables stood in front of the door and blocked his entry. The constable jerked his head questioningly at the man.

"Doctor" the man answered in one word.

The constable stepped aside and let him enter.

Veenu's father stopped pacing up and down and suspiciously watched the man in the white overcoat enter and approach his son.

"How is our hero doing today?" asked the doctor trying to sound cheerful and ignoring the father's scowls.

Vini smiled back at the doctor. "He is the same as before" she said.

"Let me see" said the doctor.

Vini and the sister got up from their chairs and helped turn Veenu on his side. The doctor undid the bandages on Veenu's head. A few minutes later he had completed his examination.

Vini, Veenu's sister and Veenu's mother gathered around the doctor anxiously awaiting his prognosis. Veenu's father scowled at the doctor from behind them.

"The external wounds are healing quickly" said the doctor. "We often see the Lizard Effect in comatose patients."

"The Lizard Effect?" repeated Vini quite concerned about what might be happening to Veenu.

"Yes" said the doctor. "Certain lizards go into a state of suspended animation when they are hurt. Healing is faster in that state especially if they need to re-grow a limb. We see a similar thing in some human patients that are comatose and hence in a state of forced suspended animation. This seems to be the case with Veenu's head."

"You mean he is growing a new head?" asked Vini still concerned.

"No. No" said the doctor. "His head injuries are healing faster than normal in his comatose state."

"Oh" said Vini. Apparently the Lizard Effect was a good thing.

"But" said Vini voicing everybody's real concern. "Will he? Will he come out of the coma?"

The doctor looked grave. "One can't say for sure" he said. "We don't know much about the brain and how it heals."

Everybody in the room looked close to tears.

"Sometimes" said the doctor "things work out." He looked around. "One must not give up hope" he said and walked out hurriedly.

———◆———

Vini had managed to convince the doctors to strictly ban all visitors for Veenu except for immediate family. She knew that if there was any leniency in this rule all sorts of people such as reporters, ministers, social activists, hunger strikers, publicity seekers and other well wishers would descend on Veenu en masse and create a constant ruckus in his room. The only way to prevent this was to completely ban all visitors no matter how important they considered themselves to be. The doctors had agreed with Vini and issued a general dictat that visitors were likely to have unknown detrimental effects on Veenu's chances of recovery and were therefore strictly forbidden. But Thang Wu had been calling Vini four times a day asking about the health of his friend and really wanted to come and see him. Vini had finally agreed to ask the doctors if they would grant special permission for him to come and see Veenu "but only for a short while" she had added "and make sure you don't get emotional while in Veenu's room. It is important to remain cheerful. I am sure Veenu can sense what is going on in the room."

Thang Wu was eternally grateful to Vini for allowing him this special privilege. "Thank you" he said.

"You are welcome" Vini replied. "I am sure Veenu will be happy to see you too."

"Thank you" said Thang Wu again.

"You are welcome" said Vini automatically.

"Thank you" said Thang Wu.

To cut a long story short, Thang Wu was now on his way to see Veenu.

It was about six in the evening. The sun was about to set. A man with a muscular frame was walking down the corridor towards Veenu's room. The *signature suspense tune* had started.

The muscular man emerged from the dark corridor into the dim light outside Veenu's room. It was Thang Wu! One of the constables moved in front of Veenu's door and jerked his head at Thang Wu.

Thang Wu was not familiar with this technique of determining a man's identity. He nodded.

The constable jerked his head again. This time it was a much more exaggerated jerk.

Thang Wu nodded his head vigorously.

The second constable realized that this was a difficult customer. He decided to help out. He moved in front of the first constable and jerked his head.

Seeing two figures of authority in front of him, Thang Wu bowed deeply.

"Not allowed to enter" said the second constable once Thang Wu had finished his bow.

"But" said Thang Wu deeply hurt. "I am special guest."

"Not allowed to enter" said the first constable firmly.

Vini had been waiting for Thang Wu. She heard the sounds outside and opened the door.

"It's ok" she said to the constables. "You can let him in."

The constables stepped aside and let Thang Wu enter.

"Thank you" he said to Vini.

But then he looked at Veenu lying completely motionless, the oxygen mask on his face and the monitor next to him showing his pulse and going 'beep' at regular intervals.

Thang Wu's eyes filled with tears. He started shaking.

"Please, Mr Thang Wu San" said Vini alarmed. "Control yourself."

"Yes" said Thang Wu. He took out a big folded handkerchief from his pocket. He opened it up completely, covered his full face with it and blew his nose loudly into it. He then wiped his eyes with it.

"Solly" he said, quickly changing his expression back to an inscrutable one.

Veenu's sister had got up from her seat next to Veenu's bed when Thang Wu had entered. She was now looking at Thang Wu rather disgustingly. Veenu's father had stopped his pacing and was scowling, his dirtiest scowl ever at Thang Wu. Vini quickly introduced Veenu's sister to Thang Wu to distract his attention from Veenu.

"This is Veenu's sister" she said.

Thang Wu bowed deeply.

Veenu's sister bowed back embarrassed.

"You vely gleat sistel of vely gleat man" said Thang Wu. He pointed at Veenu. "Him vely gleat man" he said. "He gave my watch back."

Veenu's sister looked puzzled.

Thang Wu extended his hand forward towards her to show her the watch on his wrist. He still had the handkerchief in his hand. Veenu's sister drew back a step.

"This watch" said Thang Wu. "This is a vely impoltant watch."

"Thank you" he said looking at Veenu with admiration and choking up again. "And then, he saved my plime ministel!" He paused to blow his nose again. "Thank you. Thank you."

Vini was getting irritated. "Mr Thang Wu San" she started.

"Oooooh" interrupted Thang Wu pointing his handkerchief at Veenu.

"What?" said Vini in a short voice.

"His eyes" said Thang Wu.

Veenu's mother rushed over. Everybody looked hopefully at Veenu but his eyes were still serenely closed. There was no sign of any movement.

"Veenu" said Vini softly.

There was no answer.

"Veeenu" she tried again.

There was still no answer. Veenu's father glared at Thang Wu. Veenu's sister also glared at him. She looked very much like her father when she glared.

"The doctor had given you permission to visit only for five minutes" she said firmly to Thang Wu. "Your time is up. I am afraid you will have to leave. Thank you for coming to visit."

Thang Wu bowed deeply to her.

"Thank you" he said. He left the room.

They all watched him go. The door shut gently as Thang Wu left.

"Has he gone?" said a voice from behind Veenu's sister. She jumped.

They all ran to Veenu's side. His eyes were open now. For the first time in three days, Veenu's father had a smile on his face.

"Thang Wu was right" said Vini. "Did you see him?"

"Yes, but I was afraid he would say thank you again if he felt I could hear him."

Veenu's sister laughed. His mother was crying unabashedly.

<hr />

It was dark outside. The Lava Crater Head Man was in his hotel room. He was watching TV! His gun was lying casually on the desk next to him. The TV screen was again showing the crowd outside Manilal hospital, live. The words "Breaking News" flashed red and bold on the TV screen. They were being taken back to the studios. A smiling news anchor came on.

"We have just received news that Veenu has come out of his coma!" The doctors had called for a press conference which was about to start in a few minutes. The good news was relayed to the crowd outside the hospital. A big cheer broke out. Within minutes the scene changed to one of street celebrations. People were dancing to the beat of drums which had appeared as if out of thin air. Crackers were being burst. The Lava Crater Head Man could hear the sound of crackers outside his hotel too.

The Lava Crater Head Man stood up. He walked over to the cupboard and opened it. A green nurse's uniform was hanging inside. He took it out. He opened his briefcase. There were some papers in it. He lifted them out. The briefcase was now empty. He turned the handle of the briefcase by 90 degrees. The bottom of the briefcase opened up slightly. He put his fingers under it and lifted the bottom. It was a false bottom. Underneath it was another compartment. The green nurse's uniform was placed into this compartment. The gun followed. He turned the handle back to its normal position and clicked the false bottom shut. The papers went back into the briefcase. He was ready to go.

A little while later the Lava Crater Head Man was entering Manilal hospital. He handed over his briefcase to the ladies who were inspecting the packages and passed through the metal detector without causing it to beep. A lady opened his briefcase, cursorily rummaged through it and handed it back. He was past that minor hurdle.

The *signature suspense tune* had started. The Lava Crater Head Man was walking down the dark corridor towards Veenu's room dressed in a green nurse's uniform. He emerged into the dim light in front of Veenu's room. A constable moved in front of the door and jerked his head at him.

"Nurse" said the Lava Crater Head Man.

The constable moved aside.

At that moment, Veenu was sitting up in his bed having some soup. Vini and Veenu's family were sitting next to him. Veenu's father had a lot of questions about his son's recent escapades but had been asked not to bother Veenu with questions just yet. He had managed to keep himself quiet with a great deal of difficulty.

"Oh" said Veenu suddenly and dropped his soup spoon.

All four people around him jumped up from their seats. They looked alarmed. Veenu pointed to the door. They all looked towards it.

The Lava Crater Head Man had just walked in! He looked menacing. He started to advance towards the bed. Vini and Veenu's sister both moved protectively between Veenu and the Lava Crater Head Man.

"Welcome" said Veenu from behind them.

Both the girls turned around to look at Veenu. He was smiling. Vini looked confused.

"Meet CIA agent…Ummm, I don't know your name" said Veenu to the Lava Crater Head Man who was quite close to the bed now.

The Lava Crater Head Man smiled back at Veenu. "When did you figure out that I am from the CIA?"

"It was a possibility" said Veenu "that first came into my head that morning when I finally realized that the Japanese Prime Minister was going to be blown up inside the Innovator. But I became sure only when you walked in just now."

The Lava Crater Head Man looked puzzled. It was time for some explanations.

"Well" said Veenu, "the IP address that the bomb computers were communicating with was 77.5.18.13. That's an IP address from Germany."

"Yes" nodded the Lava Crater Head Man. "We traced it to a free anonymizing VPN service provider."

"I realized then" said Veenu "that the terrorist who was watching TV waiting for the right moment to give the detonate command to the bombs need not be in Bangalore or even in India. He could be watching the right channel over the internet, just like we were, from anywhere in the world. All he needed was a good internet connection. This was not a suicide bomber or a terrorist who wanted to get himself arrested. So it would be foolish for him (or her) to be in India at the time the bombs went off. Just about every law officer in the country would be looking for him once the bombs went off and it would be harder for him to leave the country *after* the incident. So, I was sure that he would have left the country *before* the incident."

Veenu paused for breath.

"So when you just walked in, it ruled you out as the terrorist. Moreover if you were one of the terrorists, you would not have walked in here and risked getting caught.

The Lava Crater Head Man looked impressed.

"So, if you were not one of the terrorists and therefore not trying to kill me that night at the restaurant then why did you kill the Software Engineer? The answer is that the person I assumed to be a Software Engineer was not really a software engineer. He was an assassin sent to kill me! But luckily you were around to protect me!"

Veenu paused. "Thank you" he said.

The Lava Crater Head Man beamed. "You are welcome" he said. "The 'Software Engineer' was a known assassin. He had killed at least six people before. You were to be just another victim for him. He followed you out when you left the restaurant. I followed behind him. The dark, deserted street you were walking on was a great spot for the murder. I caught him when he ran towards you with the knife. He got killed in the scuffle. I only felt sorry because I would rather have taken him alive and pumped him for information."

Veenu nodded. "You were photographing him and not me, that night at the restaurant?" It was half a statement and half a question.

"Yes" said the Lava Crater Head Man. "I suspected he was the assassin, I was thinking off but needed a positive ID. So I photographed him and sent the photo to headquarters. They ran face recognition software on it and sent me back a positive confirmation!"

Veenu continued. "You were photographing an assassin at the restaurant, followed him out of there and were not afraid to scuffle with him in the dark even though he had a knife. You were clearly a trained agent. So the next question was – which agency? Then I remembered the newspaper headline I had seen in Vini's room the first time I had met her."

Veenu's mind flashed back to the scene. There was a newspaper lying on Vini's table. The headline was "US warns of terrorist threat to IT infrastructure".

"US intelligence had clearly shared some information with India based on internet chatter that they regularly monitor. That meant that you were most likely from the CIA." Veenu concluded.

The Lava Crater Head Man nodded. "This time the intelligence was strong enough for them to send me off to Bangalore to follow up on the ground" he said.

"That is why you were at ITPL photographing stuff" said Veenu. "And then again at Electronic City. That kind of behavior points to either a tourist crazy about Bangalore's software industry, a terrorist trying to stake things out for an attack or an agent trying to stake things out to protect from an attack."

"Yes" said the Lava Crater Head Man. "Unfortunately our information was not specific about a particular target or a particular date for the attack." He looked keenly at Veenu and finally asked the question he had come here to ask. "It was a clever plot. How did you figure it out?"

"The clues were all there from the beginning" said Veenu "but I was foolish enough not to put two and two together until my subconscious did it for me while I was sleeping on the day before the attack."

"The first clue were the Corn Systems' computers which were so heavy that they required an integrated wheeled base so they would not attract attention by seeming too heavy to the handlers. It was the additional weight of the integrated bombs inside that made them so heavy. And why were computers being delivered to a company that had shut down? Then that first day when I was at the Corn Systems' reception, I saw the blinking LED lights from the internet router casting eerie shadows on the glazed glass door leading to the room inside. The blinking lights indicated internet activity. Again, why was there internet activity from the computer room of a company that was supposed to have been shut down and where nobody was working? For a fleeting moment, I had even seen the shadow of a person inside the office. I had dismissed that incongruity from my head at the time but there was definitely somebody in there. He was probably setting up the computers that were being delivered in batches. I had seen the last batch outside before entering!"

"And the guard that loved to sleep." Veenu closed his eyes as he thought of the guard. "Is he dead?" he asked.

"Yes" the Lava Crater Head Man nodded. "The bomb exploded right next to him. Death was instantaneous. He died in his sleep."

Veenu sighed. "My fault" he said. "I forgot about the 21st computer lying outside on the reception table. It was the same as all the other computers. We did not kill the bomb program on that one."

"Thanks to you and Vini" said the Lava Crater Head Man. "That was the only computer which exploded. That was not enough to bring down the building or to kill the Japanese Prime Minister below. You saved the world! But that explosion was enough to kill the guard and to blow up the wall separating the reception from the main computer room. Part of that wall landed on your head!"

Veenu winced. His head still hurt when he thought about it. He closed his eyes again and said a silent prayer for the deceased guard. "He loved to sleep and is resting in peace now" said Veenu. "I don't think that it was a coincidence that the guard was always sleeping. I think they specifically chose someone like that for the job. That way they could go in and out of a supposedly shut down facility without arousing the guard's suspicion. Putting all that in the context of the newspaper headline about the terrorist threat to IT infrastructure, and I was sure of the exact infrastructure that was under threat!"

"Then the other events started to make some sense. There had been at least one attempt to kill me when the guy with the noose had shown up at my door. And if that was an assassination attempt against me, the previous night's incident was probably also a botched attempt to kill me. But why? Had I seen something, I should not have? I think the 'shadow' inside the room on my first day in Corn Systems' office saw me looking at him and perhaps believed that I had seen and understood more than I had. If I had raised the alarm early enough, a bomb squad could have opened up those computers and diffused them. Ironically, the assassination attempts are likely what caused my subconscious mind to try and figure out what was going on. Had they not tried to kill me, their plan would have succeeded!"

"Then there was the mysterious suicide of one of the founders of Corn Systems. He had apparently hung himself. My guess is that he was killed, killed by a noose. A murder that was made to look like a suicide, probably committed by the same assassin that had tried to strangle me! If Thang Wu had not intervened, I too would have been found hanging from the ceiling with a fake suicide note lying beside me."

"If Suresh Sharma had been killed by the same guy that was trying to kill me, it was probably because he had stumbled upon the same secret that I was presumed to be privy to – that bombs were integrated into the Corn Systems' computers and that the Innovator was going to be blown up."

"All this made me quite certain that the Innovator was going to be blown up. But when? My dream pointed me to the Japanese Prime Minister in addition to the Innovator. Was that random or was it intuition? Was my subconscious trying to tell me something? Where had I seen the Japanese Prime Minister before? Then I remembered. I had seen him on TV while switching channels on the first day while waiting for Vini to go out for dinner. If I remembered correctly, he was going to visit Bangalore soon. I switched on the TV and discovered that the Japanese Prime Minister was indeed going to be visiting Bangalore. In fact he was visiting that day! His first stop would be ITPL! If a terrorist was going to blow up the Innovator, what better time could they find than when the Japanese Prime Minister with the honorable Chief Minister of Karnataka in tow were inside it?"

Everybody around had been listening intently to Veenu's narration. They were all impressed.

"Wow" said the Lava Crater Head Man.

"Brilliant!" said Vini.

"Your brain still works!" said Veenu's sister.

Veenu's father nodded.

"Tell me" said Vini. "Did you know that the bombs would be detonated over the internet and all the protections that were in place to prevent them from being de-activated?"

"No" said Veenu. "I figured that out only after we reached there."

"When you knew that the Japanese Prime Minister was going to be blown up in the Innovator" said the Lava Crater Head Man, "did you inform the police?"

Veenu nodded. "Yes, I called up the Chief Inspector" he said. "But he felt that all precautions had already been taken and there was really nothing more they could do in terms of tightening security further. I have to admit that the security *was* pretty tight. It would have been pretty much impossible to smuggle in any bombs that day and get them close enough to the Japanese Prime Minister to do any damage. And based on warnings from the CIA, security had been pretty tight in the last few days also. Every piece of hardware was being scanned and switched on to check that it really was a working computer. The Corn Systems computers must also have been switched on and verified to be working computers before they entered but these were integrated computers and bombs so that check did not help."

"Yes" the Lava Crater Head Man completed the story. "Those computers were an ingenious piece of work. The bombs inside were made to look like normal computer components and did not raise any flags during the x-ray scan either. The Chief Inspector here is really a very well meaning, dedicated and competent person."

Both Vini and Veenu looked unconvinced. This assertion about the Chief Inspector seemed to be a stretch given their experience with him.

The Lava Crater Head Man continued. "Based on your description of me, he did track me down and arrest me!"

"He did?!" Veenu was surprised.

The scene flashed back to the time in the Chief Inspector's office when the Lava Crater Head Man had asked to be left alone with the Chief Inspector. The Lava Crater Head Man was opening his briefcase. He took out some papers from the briefcase and showed them to the Chief Inspector. These included the Lava Crater Head Man's ID card and other papers that proved that he was a CIA agent.

"We exchanged notes" said the Lava Crater Head Man. "The Chief Inspector had managed to track down the identity of the dead Software Engineer from his fingerprints and knew that he was really an assassin and that whoever killed him might have done it in self defense."

"Then why did he arrest me?" wondered Veenu aloud.

"He did not really arrest you" said the Lava Crater Head Man. "He just tried to scare you a bit. He found you quite irritating! From your description of the 2nd assassin, the one that tried to strangle you with a noose, he had already guessed that it was probably the man known in security circles as the Hangman."

"Why did he not listen to me when I called him and told him that the Japanese Prime Minister was going to be blown up in the Innovator?"

"That was a bit of misplaced over confidence" said the Lava Crater Head Man. "The Chief Inspector was already aware of a possible threat to the Japanese Prime Minister's life so that was not news to him. He just did not believe that it could happen at ITPL given all the precautions that had already been taken. He believed that although there was a credible security threat, the fact that intelligence was aware of it and had taken all the necessary precautions had caused the terrorists to decide not to go through with their plan."

"In fact I am guilty of believing that too" continued the Lava Crater Head Man. "The pattern of chatter on the internet was similar to previous instances where timely warnings and subsequent tightening of security had caused the terrorists to not go through with their plans. It is too risky for them to try and carry out a plan when they feel that we are on to them. That is one of the reasons we issue public warnings when there is a credible threat even though it often causes a bit of panic in the public. I guess in this case we got it wrong."

Veenu nodded. "Have you traced Sammy Batra, the other founder of Corn Systems yet? He looks like he must have been the mastermind behind this."

The Lava Crater Head Man shook his head. "He has been very clever" he said. "He went through an anonymizing VPN server in Germany to access the internet. They don't keep records so that was a dead end. We don't know where he is now. His real name is Salim Bakra. It looks like he founded Corn Systems just to execute the elaborate plan to blow up that building in ITPL. He reached out to Dr. Suresh Sharma who was passionate about technology. Suresh was only too happy to know that Sammy Batra believed in his technology and was willing to fund him and build a company based on his technology. Salim Bakra's plan was to have real employees like you working on real technology development guided by Dr. Suresh. It would have been the perfect cover! If Salim's original plan had worked, you would have been busy coding on the Corn Systems computer oblivious to the fact that it was also a bomb and would have been one of the first to be blown up."

"But" Veenu continued on behalf of the Lava Crater Head Man "Dr. Suresh found out more than he was supposed to and the Hangman had to be called in to get rid of him."

"Yes" said the Lava Crater Head Man. "It was made to look like a suicide. At that point Salim decided that he could not deal with the employees that were soon supposed to be joining in Bangalore. He would not be able to guide them. They would wonder what was going on and he really did not want them to be hanging around fiddling with the Corn Systems computers while they had nothing to do. He was afraid you guys would find out more than you were supposed to, just like Dr. Suresh had. But he did not want you raising an alarm about the Company either, so he decided to keep you happy by paying you six month's salary and not cancelling your guest house accommodation. You thought the Company had been shut down but ITPL management did not know that. They thought the Company was functioning and still in the process of setting up its office while waiting for employees to join."

The Lava Crater Head Man paused for breath. "But don't worry" he said. "We will catch this Salim Bakra pretty soon."

"Yes" agreed Veenu. "I am sure you will. It only took you ten years to catch Osama"

The Lava Crater Head Man nodded.

There was silence for a while as everybody digested everything they had just heard.

"Farewell my friend" said the Lava Crater Head Man finally "till we meet again." He turned to go.

"Wait" said Veenu. "There is a question I have been wanting to ask you."

"Yes."

Veenu pointed to the Lava Crater Head Man's lava crater head. "Is that real?" he asked.

The Lava Crater Head Man was taken aback. "No" he said. "It's a wig!"

"It's a bit much" said Veenu.

"Yes" the Lava Crater Head Man nodded wistfully. "It *is* a bit much. Next time I will have to get a better, less obtrusive wig."

"Bye" Veenu waved.

The Lava Crater Head Man waved back. He slowly walked out of the room.

Vini had just received a text message. "Quick" she said after looking at it. "Put the TV on!"

Vini's sister hit the power on button on the remote.

"Breaking News" flashed red and bold on the screen.

"Just about an hour ago the Japanese government had announced a cash award of *twenty million yen* for Veenu" said the newsreader. "And what's more, we have just received news that both the Central government and the government of Karnataka have announced awards of one crore each for Veenu! Those announcements were made within minutes of each other. I have here with me Mr. Prasanjit Banerjee, who is a former chief secretary of the treasury and an expert in the matter of govt. grants and awards."

She turned to Mr. Banerjee. "Prasanjit" she said. "Well deserved?"

"Well deserved? Yes" said Mr. Banerjee. "But announcing an award after the Japanese have already announced an award does not have much meaning. We should have been the ones to announce the award first. Now, it looks like the government has announced these awards only as a reaction to the Japanese."

Vini switched off the TV.

"Congratulations!" she said to Veenu. "You are rich! What are you going to do with all that money?"

Veenu pondered over this new problem. "Well. A good portion of it needs to go to Thank You for all his help" he said.

"But maybe not too much" he added after a pause "otherwise we will never hear the end of his Thank Yous."

"Yes" agreed Vini. "Definitely not too much!"

"And" continued Veenu "there is a committed young man out there who needs some amount of money to buy himself a nice new car... plus good insurance for it."

Vini did not understand this one.

"Who?" she asked.

"I fell on a brand new software engineer's brand new car on my way back from my job interview" Veenu explained.

By now Vini knew Veenu well enough that she did not consider falling on people's brand new cars on the way back from job interviews too out of the ordinary for him.

"There should still be quite a bit left" she said.

"The rest I will have to share 50% with you" said Veenu.

Vini considered the offer. "Maybe 25%" she said.

"50% is better" said Veenu.

"Ok. 30%" said Vini.

A strange sound was coming from Veenu's father's throat. They all turned around. Apparently he was trying to say something.

"I am…" he said. There was a long pause. His audience waited. "I am proud of you my son" he said.

THE END
(for now)

About the Author

Ashish Vikram graduated from IIT Delhi and has been working for several years as a software professional first in the Silicon Valley in the US but mostly in the IT capital on the other side of the world, Bangalore. People he knows have been telling him that his real calling is 'making people laugh'. This book is a result of their encouragement.